What  Apocalypse?

A tongue-in-cheek adventure

By Nick James

Copyright © Nicholas Plumridge 2020

This novel is a work of fiction. Names, characters, businesses, places, events and incidents are either the products of the author's imagination or used in a fictitious manner. Any resemblance to actual persons, living or dead, or actual events is purely coincidental.

All rights reserved in all media. No part of this publication may be reproduced, stored in retrieval system, copied in any form or by any means, electronic, mechanical, photocopying, recording or otherwise transmitted without written permission from the author and/or publisher. You must not circulate this book in any format. Any person who does any unauthorised act in relation to this publication may be liable to criminal prosecution and civil claims for damages.

For permission requests, please contact: Authornickjames@yahoo.com

Find out more about the author and upcoming books online at www.thebooksofnickjames.com

TheBooksofNickJames on Facebook or via Twitter @NickJam50890643

Also by the Author

The Misplaced Man: Who is in charge of his destiny?

Chasing the Dragon (The Misplaced Man Book 2)

Fallen Dynasties (The Misplaced Man Book 3)

The Victorian Vampire

"I see a tongue! Some asshole is licking my peephole." — Mark Tufo, Zombie Fallout

Authors Note

Welcome to my fifth book and I hope you have enjoyed reading my books as much as I have in writing them. Just a little warning about the character in this book- He is antisocial, a loner and as a single man in his thirties he tends to have no brain filter, so what he thinks he says. We all know people like this, and if you add a highly stressful situation into the mix they seldom shine. I hope you enjoy the book. Nick James

Chapter 1

My name is Tony Anderson. Or, if you are of the online gaming fraternity, I am Tony the Terrible. I know – scary, right? I am a thirty-year-old single male (shocker, but I did mention online gaming), and this is the story of how I tried my best to survive the Zombie Apocalypse. No, I am not Arnie, seven feet tall and ripped. I'm five feet eight tall, slightly paunchy, with the running speed of an asthmatic turtle with a limp. My odds of surviving should not have been favourable, but here is my story.

High Wycombe, Bucks

Friday 1800 hrs 12/07/2019

'It's party time, bitches!' I shouted as I walked into the two-bedroom flat, which was all mine. How, I hear you ask? Particularly as I am still in the prime of my life. Well, the unfortunate event was that my parents, who had always been of the carefree and daredevil lifestyle kind of people, died at an 'Adults only' event in the Bahamas. Trust me, you don't want to know the details.

As a result of their unfortunate passing, I inherited their flat on Corporation Road in glorious High Wycombe – the jewel of Buckinghamshire, I once heard it described as. Then again, in another breath, I'd heard it called nothing but a cess pool of evil and debauchery. Take your pick. Those of us who live, or have lived, here know the truth. But, in the end, the property is mine and, thanks to Mummy and Daddy's life insurance, I wouldn't have to work again for many a year – and after reading their post-mortem results, I would never sleep again, either.

I guess you're thinking that I am quite a callous man, who should be grieving his parents' death rather than celebrating the fact. Well, bollocks. I always felt I was a hindrance to their lifestyles. And so, as soon as I was old enough to stay home alone, they were gone. Sometimes, it would be for a whole year. And, as there were no kindly grandparents still alive to look after me and hold me to their breast while telling me that they loved me – or, to a lesser extent, tolerant aunties and uncles – I was stuck on my own.

So, when my parents died, I did mourn. Then I pulled myself together and emptied the house of all their clothes and a huge amount of marital aids, the mere sight of which scarred me for life. I dumped them all in my neighbour's bin, who still gets odd looks from the bin men. I may revisit this topic in the future in my many ramblings, but let's just say that how my late parents ever managed to walk straight legged is beyond me.

My light and breezy flat is on the third floor, just off the High Street of the Cess Pool. And said Cess Pool is a hilly town that I can view from my many windows: from the sun setting, to lightning storms, to the woman changing in the apartment opposite. Also, the property has a nice big security door that stops all the fun-loving gangster types, the permanently thirsty drunks, and the copulating homeless people settling there. It was never a good thing having to step over a clearly-in-love couple rutting on your doorstep, gender unknown, and the odours that should never be identified. It's a sight I don't want to remember… ever.

Oh, yeah, and did I mention that I have a maid? It's awesome. The downside is that she's a very angry person, and she refuses to let me buy her a uniform. She says she's a cleaner not a maid. Maybe I did overstep the employer/employee boundary, but if you don't ask you don't get.

So as I danced down the hallway, sending my shoes flying into the shoe-gathering corner. I headed into the kitchen and took out an ice-cold can of pop. Thankfully, for a few more pounds a week cash in her lovely, slender hand, Olga the Russian angry maid – and possible ex-KGB – willingly filled my kitchen with all the foodstuffs I required to maintain my god-like physique. Even though her rough exterior showed me nothing but distain, I truly believed that she was starting to warm to me, and that one day, far far in the future, maybe this would be true love. Had this been Disney, I would be dancing with a sewer rat called Alfred. Anyway, enough about my love life. *Cough.*

The can hissed as I opened it, freeing the pent-up pressure back to the world that unjustly contained it. It was like nectar to a bee. I placed the condensation-coated can onto a coaster – after all, I am no slob. Like a well-honed hitman, I knew where all my tools were. With a flick of my right hand, I pressed a button and my recliner put me at ease in the feet-up, head-back position. Not too far – just enough to be relaxed and still see the television without straining my neck.

With my left hand, I summoned my phone like a bespectacled wizard who had a thing for ginger friends. We do not judge him, or we shall be judged also. I pressed button number one on the pre-set list and waited.

'Hello, Dragon Pizzas, how can I help you?' came an angelic voice, the owner of which instantly claimed my heart as her own. Please carry my first born, my love.

'Hiya, Kimberley, how's tricks?'

There was a brief silence. 'Oh, hi Tony. I saw you walk past earlier,' Kimberly, the raven-haired goddess, purred at me. 'Not like you to walk anywhere?'

I had to come up with a lie quickly. 'I went to the gym,' I said and doffed my cap to quick-thinking Tony, giving myself a mental high five.

Once again, there was that pause. 'Is that a guy called Jim, or the place where people go to exercise?' she asked with cold tones. This little kitty cat had claws. *Meow*.

'The latter, my dear,' I said in my best Mr Darcy tones.

And that's when the laughter started and didn't stop for quite a while. Something told me she didn't believe me. 'Okay, Tony,' she said, 'where did you *really* go?'

I groaned inwardly. *Damn women and their mind-reading capabilities.* 'I heard that the Burger King was being reopened, but it was a lie.' With that, the floodgates of mocking laughter burst free once again.

After about five minutes, she came back to the phone. 'The usual Friday order, Tony?' the Devil woman asked.

'Yes please, Kimberly,' I replied in a deflated tone. My confidence, which was always slightly lacking, finally gave up the ghost and took flight.

'Cheer up, chuckles. Dinesh will bring it over in about twenty minutes. I'll put it on your tab, hun,' Kimberly said, reclaiming part of my heart.

'I'll even throw in some onion rings for the laugh.' The call disconnected, leaving me alone with her laughter still ringing in my ears. But they say that if you can make a woman laugh, that's half the job. Sorted.

Thirty minutes later, fat, grease and various meat products entered my system and I began to relax after my testing day. I watched my favourite childish cartoon, which made me roar with laughter as I consumed my feast. Afterwards, I swept away all the evidence of my lack of healthy living straight into the bin, ready for Olga to dispose of on Monday, when I would run away and hide, so I didn't have to listen to her insults in English and Russian. I do have feelings, after all.

As the night wore on, I flicked through the channels. The news was to be avoided, as usual. All they seemed to talk about was doom and gloom. Sod that – I have that outside my front door. I don't need to know what is happening in Europe. Xbox, here we come.

As I was storming the beaches of Normandy – I know it's a game, so shut up – I thought about something I had been meaning to try. I won't say where I heard or read about it, and I always hoped I would try it with a long-term girlfriend who liked to push the boundaries. Once again, don't judge me. It's called riding the bull. You mix Viagra – not that I need it (that's right, ladies) – with a couple of cans of Red Bull (or any other brand of energy drink, but Red Bull sounds better). I put on some adult entertainment that just so happened to be in my DVD player, swallowed the little blue pill and then the two cans of rocket fuel.

I sat there in comfort as I had changed into my typical shorts and T-shirt, the latter telling the world 'I liked the Family Guy'. I watched as some freakishly big man delivered a pizza to a small-in-stature, but large-in-chest woman, who was sitting in nothing but her underwear reading a book. I hoped it had small words like this. Disappointment crept in slightly as only the canned drink seemed to be working. *Oh… hang on. What's this?* I thought to myself as my body started to tingle.

'AARGH!' I screamed as my body went rigid and pain burst out like a firework from my chest. Then there was nothing but darkness, and the sound of some woman complaining about how her hair was now sticky.

High Wycombe, Bucks

Saturday 0900 hrs 13/07/2019

'No pineapple on mine,' I mumbled, having finally awoken from my pizza and drug-fuelled sleep. My body was stiff as a board. Clearly, the Viagra worked on my entire body, not just my little gangster.

Sunlight filtered through my thin curtains, enabling me to see the dust particles floating in the air. I looked around and realised the television was on standby and that, clearly, whatever I had dreamt about the night before had added to my need to shower, and possibly burn my boxers. Unfortunately, too many things had relaxed on me last night. Thank small mercies for the Scotch Guard I had sprayed on my chair. While I had unknowingly secreted certain substances from my body, I wondered whether Olga would kindly come and clean my chair for me.

I stilled at the thought of the tall, slim, very stoic ex-Russian national giving me another lecture about me being a pig as a result of her finding a rogue Monster Munch on the floor. Hence the reason why, since that day, I left the safety of my flat to escape her lectures. Luckily, that meant that on Mondays, Wednesdays and Fridays I got some fresh air as I walked to the KFC, TGI or any other place that would happily give me asylum for a few hours away from the blonde-haired giantess.

After a thorough shower, I was clean and walked around my kingdom naked with the towel wrapped around my dark locks. I did find out where that secretive maid kept the cleaning products, but as I read the labels I realised I should've studied harder at school. Clearly, one needed a higher education to understand these bloody things and what they did. In frustration, I launched Mr Sheen down the hallway.

'Sod it, that'll do,' I mumbled as I placed my seat cushion in the shower cubicle and covered it in the chosen fluid. It smelt potent, so I figured it should do a good enough job, and I scrubbed the cushion with water from the shower head. I was worried about three things at this moment in time. One, the burning sensation on my hands. Two, the fumes, which were building up and were a tad pungent for my virginal undamaged lungs. Three, my once lovely dark brown cushion was now turning white.

I picked up the blue bottle and read the label: *Domestos bleach*. Bleach cleans things... right? I truly don't understand this world. How bad can it be, for God's sake? You put it down the toilet and you sit on it. Why would it destroy fabric?

'For fuck's sake!' I started to take my frustrations out on anything that I could find. Take that, towelling robe.

I chose to close the bathroom door with the shower going, hoping to be able to turn back time on my stupidity, though I was still not sure what I had done wrong. I'd leave Olga a note and ask for her advice. Or maybe just buy a new chair? That'll be safer.

Then, what suddenly hit me was that, this morning, there was an ominous absence of noise – not just in the flats, but also outside. So, like a hero, I put on a CD and let M People serenade me as I donned some new duds for a full night of doing nothing – apart, that is, from waging war against the dark forces of the axis of evil. Normandy, here we come.

'Oh, come on!' I screamed at my TV as the body of my character was separated from his cherished limbs. 'Come on, walk it off, buddy. You can do it!'

Just then, a loud noise shook the whole flat. I knew I hadn't caused the noise as I had turned off my sub-woofer after Mrs Martínez had started shouting at me in the corridor at 3 am one morning. It wasn't my fault she'd bought the flat beneath mine. Opening the door, I had seen that she was in her sleepwear. What amazed me was the fact the fifty-something woman didn't realise that the hall light made her nightdress translucent, which gave me a front-row centre view of the perfect picture of womanhood. To be honest, I didn't say a lot back to her – maybe a couple of clicks and whistles – and then she stomped off. I did something else more pleasant in the dark, alone.

Then came another boom and I heard the windows rattle, which wasn't a good sign. Being a lazy sod, my curtains were still closed. I jumped up from my unsoiled sofa, drew back the curtains and looked out.

'What the fuck...' I muttered quietly, so that only my dying cheese plant would hear, as I took in the smoke-filled view. Flames and smoke billowed out from over the rooftops opposite. My first instinct was that the nearby petrol station had gone up in flames. It was run by a friendly Sri Lankan couple. I hoped that they were okay. I could see people in the distance running and walking down the high street. Closing the curtains, I tried to gather my wits, and my breath, in an attempt to calm down.

I took a drink from the fridge, pulled out a chair and sat at my glass top dining table. It was designed for four people, but the only people that had been in this flat were me, Olga and a takeaway delivery driver, who had turned up early and had spilled the beans to my Russian maid about how much junk food I consumed. In my defence, I had hoped she would have left by the time the food was due to arrive, but once again that led to a long, one-sided discussion about my health and poor diet.

Anyway, I opened my laptop – at least the internet was still working. With a quick thought about the future, I scrubbed my browser history clean. Better safe than sorry.

I looked at the news feed and there it was, plastered all over the bloody screen.

'How the hell…?' I scoffed, hoping it was all a joke as I read the news headlines: PANDEMIC, INFECTED WATER, INFECTED FOODS, TERRORISM, THE DEAD WALK, ZOMBIES, RICHARD GERE MARRIES A… STAY IN YOUR HOMES.

My mind was racing. I had walked around the district only yesterday, so how come I'd never heard about all this? According to the reports, it began in Europe and, thanks to international flights, it had spread quickly by exchange of fluids (chance would be a fine thing) or from being bitten. That was according to the *Guardian* website, which I seldom read. I know – surprising, right?

Firstly, when the infection took hold, some people just fell ill. Some died and some didn't. Then, the dead rose up again a day later and started to feast on people. Another site said that some just bit and ran, to spread the infection quicker. However, the world armed forces had now been activated and were starting to fight back, though the infection was spreading quicker than they could react.

I rubbed the tears away from my face. I had been so clueless. While I was walking around, all happy, families in other parts of the world were being killed by their friends or family. And now it was in England, but it came to us threefold: via air transport, the Channel Tunnel, and ferries.

I closed the laptop screen. I didn't want to know anything else. My pulse was racing like a Grand Prix car, so I headed to bed and hoped that, when I came back out, it would all be fixed, and Olga would shout at me for ruining my chair. I hoped she was okay. Once again, sleep claimed me as my system shut down to protect itself.

Chapter 2

High Wycombe, Bucks

Sunday 0700 hrs 13/07/2019

'The Man of Iron, Tony Anderson, aka Tony the Terrible, woke up and walked from his bed, where he had just spent the last few hours laying waste to many maidens' virginity...' I monologed as I walked towards the closed curtains. I placed my hands on the curtains and paused before casting them aside, hoping all the time that it had been a dream, or that the camouflaged units of Her Majesty's armed forces would be fighting tooth and nail to reclaim the island back from the infected/dead.

I threw the curtains apart and saw flames, smoke and the dead. *Crap*. I watched as hordes of what were once people lumbered slowly up the high street. Even below the flats, I could see people, as well as bodies on the ground. My eyes locked onto a corpse that had been torn open.

'Oh, Kimberly, that's just not right,' I muttered. I saw several other bodies scattered around her. Clearly, they had grouped together for safety when the shop was attacked.

My body went limp and my stomach flipped as I thought about the sassy pizza clerk who had bantered with me on so many occasions. Stomach acid began burning away the lining as I fought to keep from retching. The world was coming to an end – which was how Wycombe looked at the best of times, but it was never this bad.

I rushed to the kitchen and gulped down some water. Thankfully, the services were still on – power and water for now. My Olga-stocked cupboards were still full, but that wouldn't last long. I grabbed some cereal and the last of the milk – but that didn't matter, as cereal is good, wet or dry. I headed back into the lounge and opened the laptop. The news feed had slowed down. It appeared that things out east had gone black – using the American military slang that the media love to use. Where's Stormin' Norman when you need him?

The groans and wails from outside were beginning to filter through the walls, and it was starting to upset my calm. It was just like in the movies. They must have either seen me at a window, or sensed my desperation or fear. Maybe the bleached and ruined chair cushion that I had lost my temper with and thrown into the street had caught their attention? Okay, so that was it.

As the hours ticked away, I watched zombie flick after zombie flick. The closest one to my situation was *Sean of the Dead*. And no, I don't have any cornettos, a cricket bat or a girlfriend. I had to focus; everything was going to shit. I took a leaf out of Matt Damon's tactics in *The Martian* and made a list of all the available foodstuffs. Honestly, how many times does that man need to be rescued? And that's when my conversations with Olga came back to haunt me. Twenty-four cans of pop, two multi-packs of Monster Munch, a few bars of Snickers, and that was it. All the frozen meals and ice lollies had been eaten. If I was honest with myself, things weren't looking good for this kid.

I tried to shake off the wave off melancholy that threatened to smother me.

'Get yourself together, Tony,' I chided myself and rushed off to shave and shower. Might as well, for who knew when that might stop working?

The block of flats was so quiet, almost like a tomb. I chewed my bottom lip as I paced. There were four flats per level, with three levels, making twelve flats in total. The main building had big security doors front and back, both with coded locks. I headed to my front door, despite what my head was telling me to do – to run and hide, mainly. But I needed more food and any bottled water.

I unlocked my door and eased it open. Luckily for me, being a new build there wasn't a single creak from door or floor. I snuck to the top of the stairs and looked down to the first floor. Seeing nothing down there, I slowly continued my journey downwards. Like everywhere in the building, the stairs had fitted carpets, so my trainers never made a sound, all bar the odd creak from the metal edging on the stairs themselves.

My nerves were as taut as piano wire. I could hear them thrum as I stepped down to the ground floor. The noise of the dead was louder down here, their bloodied, white-eyed faces pressed up against the small window apertures of the doors. It was the same at the back. It was then that time stopped. Apart from the faces and the noise, what caused this moment of bowel-wrecking fear were the bloody handprints. But it wasn't red. There was a long, brown line of it spread across the once pristine white corridor walls to Flat 2.

So many possibilities flashed through my mind, but two main ideas were formed. The first was to run back to the flat and cry like a baby until the aliens or army came and rescued my arse. The second was to grab a sharp knife and see what was in there. So, I ran back to my flat and threw up into my toilet. I know, hardcore, right?

Soon enough, I let my hours of watching American action films dictate my decision. I took my sharpest and biggest blade from my Deadpool knife block and headed back downstairs. I wish I could say I donned my leather jacket, motorcycle gloves and heavy-duty work boots to get ready for zombie war, but that would be a total lie. I wore trainers, some loose jogging bottoms and a stained black T-shirt. Hardly SEAL Team Six or the good old SAS.

I repeated my journey down the stairs to the ground floor, and my stomach felt like it was tying itself up in knots. With every step, I felt like every waste product in my body wanted to flee. I mastered my breathing as I touched down onto the carpeted ground-floor lobby. My audience was there waiting, pawing at the doors. They looked so hopeful that I would walk on over and let them chow down on my chubby arse.

'Not today, bitches,' I muttered, but that just seemed to goad them, their dry lips peeled back over their broken teeth.

Dark thoughts clouded my brain, which I had to clear before I ventured into the flat of death. I shook my head and breathed in and out, flooding my system with oxygen. My hand moved to the door handle. In my other hand I held the large knife, ten inches of stainless steel of justice. Internally, I chuckled at the thought of the size. However, the zombie who then decided to smash his head into the toughened glass of the main door, causing him to drop like a stone, gave me the hurry up.

'Three, two, one, here I go!' I shouted and pushed the handle. As I did so, I started to move forward, smashing my head into the wooden door. 'It's fucking locked,' I said and nearly sobbed. I let my body slide down the door and onto the floor.

As I lay there on the blood-stained floor, a thought knocked. Why was I trying to get into the one flat that had a bloody zombie in it? Was it to prove to myself that I could kill to survive? Or was it because I had seen John Edwards going in carrying a crate of lager and bags of nachos the day before?

My legs managed to hold as I got up and walked to Flat 1 and knocked.

'Hello, is anyone there? It's Tony from upstairs.' Unfortunately, that made my fans outside headbutt the glass even more. 'Won't be doing that again,' I chuckled as I saw a zombie wearing a stab proof vest turning his face into pulp against the door.

I tried the handles on all the flats on the ground floor but the doors were all locked. So I headed upstairs and gave a couple of knocks and tried the door handles there. That was the trouble with Wycombe – it was the perfect commuter town, where business or individuals would rent or buy flats to use during the working week, especially as London was easy to get to. Door after door was locked, but that was no surprise, as they were all self-locking. I had one more to check on the second floor – the one and only Mrs Martínez.

Of course, the door handle went all the way down and I heard the click of the latch disengaging from the frame. My heart began racing again as I pushed the door open to her flat. Clearly, Mrs Martínez was into minimalism; the hall was bare and crisp white, with clean wooden flooring. However, there was no noise, or any signs of blood. The door closed behind me with an echoing click. I moved the knife to my dominant right hand and moved on through the plush flat. The bedroom was clear, as was the kitchen and spare room. Not a single drop of blood, or any sign of disturbance. The only noise was the pounding of my heart.

I bent down, placing my hands on my knees and took some deep breaths. It was becoming ever more apparent that I did not thrive on pressure. I know, it surprised me, too.

I went back into the kitchen to examine the contents. It appeared that the lovely Mrs Martínez had recently been shopping, as there were plenty of cans, as well as some diet drinks.

'SCORE!' I cried out as I opened a floor-level cupboard and found two cases of bottled water, twenty-four litres in total. Happy days.

The water was lugged upstairs, then I found some of the lady's forever shopping bags, which unfortunately probably outlasted said woman.

The cans and anything else I could find were put into the heavy-duty hessian shopping bag. It took a couple of trips, but at least I could stay in my flat for another couple of weeks or more. It was on my last trip that my bladder decided to make it known it was full.

I headed straight to Mrs Martínez's bathroom and opened the door. What greeted me was a room awash with blood, and then a blood-curdling groan as the owner of the property launched herself at me with teeth bared, already doing the biting motion. The lady from Spain was still wearing that nighty.

My head slammed into the hallway wall as I was driven to the floor, covered in bloody spittle. As stars shot through my vision, I managed to keep my hand on her throat, but the strength of her amazed me. Yes, I know I wasn't strong, but still. I could feel my fingernails beginning to break through the parchment-thin skin of her throat, drawing blood. However, I kept on pushing, causing her blood to trickle down my hand.

I had to get her off me. My strength was failing and, in my fatigue-riddled mind, I came up with a plan. Well, it was do or die. In a moment of hindsight, or simply my laziness, I had wedged the front door of Mrs Martínez's apartment open with one of her bean bag doorstops, but in a classic trade-off I had left the knife upstairs in my kitchen. The plan was to rock her side to side and then push her off down her clean, tidy hallway, and then run to the door and lock her in.

Well, the first part worked, as we rocked like giddy lovers would. With a grunt and a loud expletive, I threw the once beautiful woman to the floor. I think any man would be embarrassed by how far I managed to push her away from me. But hey, they were not there.

My trainers and hands struggled on the now bloody laminate flooring. I scrabbled for purchase, as did the zombie and, before she was back on her feet, I was heading down the hall and to the front door. I kicked the door stop and felt my little toe scream for mercy. The door started to close as I fell against the railing on the stairway, my momentum attempting to send me over and down to the ground floor. I managed to stop myself as my luck held. I spun round to inspect my handiwork, but all I could see was the rabid form of my neighbour coated with blood, mouth and eyes wide, throwing herself at me with her sharp nails ready to claw and gouge.

In a panic, I dropped to the ground and protected my head with both hands. However, instead of the sharp grip of teeth on my flesh, I received a knee to the head as Mrs Martínez was sent careering over the railing to the ground floor, smashing her skull on the steps below. My neighbour was now gone and at rest. And, as it so happened, my bladder was now feeling better. Make of that what you will.

I stood up unsteadily and looked down over the railing. I saw that Mrs Martínez had a blood-soaked bandage on her left wrist; clearly, she had been bitten, but had managed to get home, where she no doubt had treated herself. But it wasn't an injury that could be cured by a simple bandage. It was then that I thought about all the blood and spittle that was still coated on my face and body.

'Aww, shit,' I said to myself. The zombies outside sounded pissed. I just prayed to any deity that still existed to keep those doors closed and secure.

My shower called and I washed my body and face red raw. At least I could have some nice tinned food. I sat and watched a Disney film while eating peaches and orange segments to lighten my mood, and I waited to see if the infection would claim my life, as it had done to so many others. What would the next day bring me?

Chapter 3

High Wycombe, Bucks

A month Later. Monday time/unknown 12/08/2019

'Oops I did it again' I sang out loud as I strode down the hallway outside my flat. Yes, I was singing along to Britney Spears while doing my best catwalk strut and poses. And, possibly, I would admit that I was wearing a pair of red four-inch high heels. *Why?* I hear you ask. Well, I will tell you. What else goes with a floor-length red ball gown?

This past month had been one of the worst times ever. Yes, the world had ended. And I had killed the owner of said shoes and dress, the late and great Mrs Martínez. Whom I dragged into one of the downstairs flats, which didn't contain a zombie.

It was later in the month when the lights finally went out around the world. Either someone in authority ordered the power grid to be turned off, or a power station had gone *boom*. Thanks to my boredom and endless hours of pointless internet searches, I learnt that nuclear power stations were all positioned on the coast due to their need for water in order to cool the core.

After my haphazard attempt at breaking into the late Spanish woman's flat, I decided that I had to break into the rest, but avoiding the one with the blood-smeared door. Unfortunately, there wasn't much food in the other apartments as they were mainly just used by commuters during the week for sleeping in, but there were some tins, pasta and cereals. A good few bottles of water, too.

Also, I had collected any iPods, laptops or mobile phones that I could find and kept them all charged up. The iPods and phones were restored back to factory settings and I downloaded my own tunes onto them. That way, should the power go completely, I would still have my tunes to keep me sane, and then only until I had drained them all.

Even though I was a natural loner, as the weeks went by, not seeing any people, even in passing, began to hurt. Two of the five laptops I had procured were not password protected, and only one of them was a personal laptop. I scrolled through Mr O'Brien's family photos, felt some guilt when coming across some risqué ones of Mrs O'Brien. But what was a man to do during a zombie apocalypse?

When the darkness finally did come, I did cry out in fear and loneliness. However, my anguish was drowned out by the constant moaning and groaning of my companions outside. Normally, I wouldn't hear them, but as we were now experiencing England's two-week summer, which seemed to have extended itself just to torture me, I was now forced to open all the windows in the flat to allow air circulation. As a result, I was now party to the songs of the Zombie Choir.

The third day after the power died, I was brought to the window by the sound of screaming. I leant out the window and saw two teenagers running past the flat, with an ever-increasing horde of zombies behind them. They were running hand in hand, clearly young lovers that had been trapped somewhere. Their clothing was not helping their escape, however – baggy skater-boy jeans and boots for the shaven-headed male youth, and leggings and platform trainers for poor Juliet.

Their downfall, however, was the noise they were making. They were shouting encouragement to each other, while throwing a mixture of profanities to the crowd behind them. I could see how it was going to play out.

'No, no, no…' I muttered as they ran into another zombie group that had just appeared from around the high street. The girl was dragged down by her ponytail with a blood-curdling scream. The boy, in an act of heroism, tried to pull the animals that were feasting on his screaming girlfriend away, but he was quickly lifted off his feet by a huge male zombie. In the blink of an eye, he disappeared from sight… but not sound.

I closed my windows and hoped that God would take all my senses and let me join the world's population. And, with that thought alone, my mental health spiralled downwards. I dedicated a lot of my time to learning how to walk in the heels; it took way too much brain power to do that without falling over the railings to my death.

I had made my way downstairs as my fear-ridden brain told me that I should dance in front of my flesh-eating audience. Unfortunately, as the music was loud and my earphones were good, I didn't hear as the door was forced open. However, as I spun around, which had taken me several hours to master in the stilettos, I saw a dirty but angry face in front of me. The look of disgust he gave me was out of this world. And then, just like the power, my lights were turned out.

***

My eyes fluttered and pain shot through my brain and body. I groaned and managed to look around. I was in my flat, still sporting my very flattering red dress, though it was looking a little dishevelled. By the way my body was aching, the shit must've dragged me up here. A noise was coming from the kitchen. Clearly, the man who knocked me on my arse was turning my place over, muttering as he did so.

To say I was panicking was an understatement. I promised myself not to lose my shit, but I might have lied, and it wouldn't have been the first time.

'WHERE'S THE FUCKING BOOZE?' filtered from the kitchen. I just hoped he wouldn't eat the last of the Weetabix.

A very tall, wiry and exceptionally angry man came storming into the living room. I thought he was just going to shout at me, but he thumped me in the face again, causing blood to spray out from my smashed nose and over my cheeks and chest. The force of the punch sent me backwards, tilting the chair I was slumped in back against the wall.

Darkness fought with me to drag me in the realm of unconsciousness, though I won this time. As my eyesight struggled to regain its normal clarity, the man was pacing back and forth, still muttering. The first thing I noticed was the mass of silver, waist-long dreadlocks – not the usual thing you see on a fifty-something white man. And the fact that he hadn't blinked since he had started to walk in front of me was just plain weird.

He turned his piercing grey eyes on me again. 'You a poof?'

I frowned. 'No. Why?'

This time he did blink, but not both eyes at the same time – his right eye was about a second late. He scanned me up and down slowly. Clearly, he was bat shit crazy. He didn't say another word, but just kept on looking at me.

'What do you want?' I said. 'I have hardly any food or drink.'

His eyes pierced me straight to my soul, and once again looked me up and down. He was starting to freak me out, even more than before.

'Are you a FUCKING POOF?' the crazy bastard demanded.

'NO. WHY WOULD YOU THINK THAT?' I screamed back. I was aware of the amount of heterosexual sex I had had in my life. People could think I was gay, though, if they wanted. Who cared? Especially now.

The man pressed his dirty face even closer to mine. 'Because you're wearing a fucking dress!'

Ah, yes, I could see his point now. 'My clothes were dirty, and there was no water to clean them,' I said and mentally high-fived myself. Quick-thinking Tony. I do seem to congratulate myself a lot. Maybe it was the lack of parenting I had as a child. But let's put a pin in that for later.

The stillness in the man's features really did start to worry me. 'What about the heels? And the dancing?' *Oh fuck.*

We had a staring contest going on. Clearly it was my turn to talk, but I had nothing to say.

'What is it that you want from me?' I demanded. However, if I'd thought about it, I'd have realised that he might have a point about the signs of my questionable sexuality, but that is a conversation for another day. I guess he didn't like my question, as he sent me back to sleep.

I didn't know how long I was out, but when I awoke from my enforced slumber, thanks to the pain from my clearly busted nose, I saw the scary, mentally damaged man sleeping on my sofa, naked. That was not what I needed to see, especially as he had earlier demanded to know about my sexuality. If he tells me I have a pretty mouth, that's it – I would scuttle over to the window and attempt to throw myself, and the chair I was tied to, down to our bloody deaths. Well, mine, anyway.

My eyes closed, and this time it was not unconsciousness, but sweet slumber. Dreams of my parents filtered through my worried mind; but strangely, the nicest part of the dream was when the mighty Olga came back and began kicking the weird man out. And then she carried me out, like in the Richard Gere film *An Officer and a Gentleman*. Mum loved that movie, she always cried at the ending. Okay, I must man up.

This is getting stupid. I am a man, for fuck's sake. It says so on my birth certificate.

A ringing slap to my cheek awoke me. The freak was looming over me with my carving knife in his hand.

'Where's ya food and ya booze?' he once again demanded.

'All I have is in the bloody kitchen, I promise,' I pleaded pathetically.

Anger rippled through his features, and his unblinking eyes shot from side to side while the demons worked in his mind. Clearly, you had to be mental to survive in this world, but that didn't bode well for my survival.

'What about other flats? You check 'em?' he said.

I nodded. 'All but one of them,' I said. 'Flat One. I couldn't break into it. I'm not strong enough.' Yes, it was a lie, but hell – what else was I going to do? I had formulated a plan of sorts – to start crying like a baby until I became dehydrated, he would become disgusted with me, then I would pounce.

The man was now walking up and down the lounge, arguing with himself. Yes, I do talk to myself, but he was taking it to the extreme. Never once did I answer back to myself.

He stormed off out of the flat (I wish he would get dressed), his bare feet making no noise thanks to the carpeting. He wouldn't see any signs of a zombie being in that flat as I had washed the blood from the walls and door weeks ago, especially after Mrs Martínez had taken the drop and splattered blood everywhere. I hate cleaning, but it had started to smell funky.

The front door to my flat was kicked open and the man ran up to me. *Please, oh please don't kiss me…*

'You're coming with me, bitch!' he shouted, spraying me with God knows what he had been eating. Thank God he wasn't a dog. He untied me from the chair and dragged me with him. Small mercies I had taken off the shoes earlier. He was talking all the way down to the ground floor and I didn't understand a fucking word. He might as well have been speaking a foreign language.

He threw me down onto the now clean carpets. Olga can quit her bitching about sweeping up my Pringle crumbs. Try sweeping up a body, BITCH!! *Sorry, Olga, didn't mean it. Miss you,* I thought as the psycho was clearly trying to tell me something, but I just wasn't listening. He thrust the carving knife into my hand and pushed me away to give himself room to attack said door. Maybe I should've clarified with the crazy kidnapper/hopefully not rapist what my role in this was. Instead, I was spending my time reminiscing about Olga's shapely bum.

BANG!

She did have a nice bum, though.

BANG!

Yeah, she was a few years older than me. She had lovely honey blonde hair.

BANG!

She was always tidy…

'Fucking help me, ya POOF!' the psycho screamed. I shook myself out of my stupor, realising that he had kicked the door open to John Edwards' flat. Good on him.

The owner of Flat 1 was now sprawled upon the crazy bastard. He was screaming at me to act. The Zombie Edwards, meanwhile, was groaning loudly while trying to taste the Weetabix-eating git. I was torn in more ways than my dress at what to do. Should I help the man who wanted to do unknown things to me? Or just let the zombie eat him? What if we were the last two human beings on this planet? Should I let him die?

The more I thought about it, if we were the last surviving humans, mankind would die out anyway, and there was no way I was going to be his wife. Maybe I should have put some man clothes on.

'HELP MEEEEE!' he screamed.

The dribbling Zombie Edwards was forcing himself down closer to Mr Crazy's face. The snapping sound of the man's jaws was gut-wrenching, just like when Flynn dragged his nails down the blackboard in *Jaws*. Love that film.

But I had to save him. It was my time to be the hero and make my family proud. Finally, Tony the Terrible would earn his place on the battlefield. I spun the knife around so that I could stab down with force. I picked it back up after ballsing up the spin.

'What you fucking playing at? STAB THE BASTARD!' Mr Impatient cried.

I took a deep breath and threw myself onto the pile.

'ARRRGHHH! DIE AGAIN, YOU BASTARD!' I screamed in a butch, manly style as I stabbed the zombie repeatedly, until I was covered in the viscous, darkened blood.

I rolled off to the side, panting. I had a strange smile on my face. I had saved another, and turned to accept the hopefully forthcoming gratitude.

'Oh,' I said as I took in the sight of two dead men, not just one.

The hordes of zombies outside were banging and groaning against the glass doors as I sat there, cross-legged. When I had jumped onto the zombie's back in my attempt to be a saviour, I had inadvertently forced the maneater's face into the struggling man's neck. I sighed and blew out the breath I was holding, just as the newly dead man was coming back. It truly was like in a horror film – the milky white eyes stared into me as he stretched out with his nicotine-stained fingers.

The blade came out of Mr Edwards' skull with a disgusting slurping sound, just like the way old people drink tea out of a saucer, and I took aim. The point of the blade was so close to his eye that you could see the lens concave. I closed my eyes, counted to three and pushed as hard as I could. It was easier than I thought, but before I opened my eye I heard him moan. I opened my eyes.

'Fucker!' I exclaimed. The sod had moved and I had cut all the way down the side of his head. The knife was retrieved and, this time with my eyes open, I stabbed him in the eye, knowing he would live again in the afterlife.

I was proud of what I had done this day. I had saved myself from a possible murderer, killed two zombies, and now had another flat to plunder. And all the while wearing a red dress. Maybe Chris De Burgh was right to sing about me.

I pulled the now leaking bodies into the flat where I had deposited Mrs Martínez, just to give the owner of my dress some company, and closed the door. Everything of use had been pillaged from the flat days ago. I got on my hands and knees like an old-fashioned washer woman cleaning a doorstep of a terraced house. The blood and other badly smelling liquids were cleaned up, and then a healthy amount of bleach was applied to finally kill all that could be classed as zombie juice.

Mr Edwards was only slightly bigger than me, so first to be checked was his bedroom to find some clothes. And, just as in the annals of history Moses went up to Mount Sinai and was gifted the ten commandments, I went into Mr Edwards' bedroom cupboard drawers and was gifted with two sealed packs of boxer shorts. Praise be.

The bathroom had a myriad of wet wipes and deodorants, so this home boy was now smelling as fresh as a baby. The final thing to complete my ensemble was a combination of a plain white T-shirt and grey jogging bottoms. I felt clean once more. And quite happy that the only person to have seen me in a dress was now dead.

Chapter 4

High Wycombe, Bucks

Time - unknown. Date - who cares?

'I... HAVE... WEETABIX!' I sang as I danced around the late John Edwards' kitchen. He must have been planning a party as it was full of snacks and, thankfully, tinned food. And the prize... a case of lager. 'Sweeeeeet!' Oh, and some two-litre bottles of water. I planned to have a small gathering tonight, mainly me and the lager, as well as several bags of Kettle chips.

Thanks to John, I had a nice, fully charged laptop. I now had enough food and water for a week or two, but that just wasn't enough. I had been looking out of the windows more as of late – although, ever since the teenagers had been dragged down to their deaths, I had seen no one, not a living soul. I knew the time was coming when I would have to leave my castle – but where to?

I sat there looking through my windows while eating my newly acquired wholegrain cereal. I added the milk replacement (lager) and a liberal scattering of sugar – again, thanks to Mr Edwards. However, my eyes were looking to the horizon where smoke was filling the skies once more. This was a small, compact town in a valley, surrounded by woods. After a long, hot summer, it was far too easy for fires to spread, and I knew my time here was running out. But where to go? I couldn't drive, and I had no living members of family. Also, thanks to my anti-social mentality, I had no close friends, either.

I knew that the easiest car to drive was an automatic, but how to drive, or even find, one before the zombie hordes came crashing down upon me? There were only a few cars in the car park at the back of the flats. Unfortunately, it wasn't a gated secure area, so as soon as the key was in the ignition I would be on my way. I knew it was a risk I needed to take, especially as my food stocks had started to dwindle to dangerous levels.

Several cans of alcohol helped me to sleep that night, even though the flesh-eating rabble were getting noisier by the day. Clearly, they were also getting hungry. I searched from flat to flat and gathered all the car keys I could find. Luckily, they were in bowls or hanging up by the front doors.

I stood looking out over the car park from the second-floor window, and clicked the 'unlock' buttons on the ignition keys, just to make sure the cars would open and that there was, at least some, power.

'Result,' I said, punching the air. All three cars' headlights illuminated, indicating that there was some power in the battery.

The acid in my stomach began bubbling like a witch's cauldron as I planned my next step. First, I needed to ascertain which car was an automatic. My immediate problem, however, was the half-dozen biters situated at the back door which opened onto the said car park.

I made my way to the rear-most ground-floor flat and went into the main bedroom. Its window was facing the car park and was also farthest away from the back door of the apartment block. The drop out of the window was only three feet. Therefore, if I were to put all my ninja skills into play, I could jump down silently and run to the cars. Hopefully, one of them would be my ride out of here and freedom.

The sun was nearly gone for the day. I eased the PVC-framed window open. A security bar stopped it opening all the way, but with a slight jiggle it was released, allowing me a good view out of the front of the flat. My priority was to ensure that the biters didn't notice a thing. They were still moaning and groaning at the door. As a distraction, I had made sure that they saw me as I passed the door to the flat. Even in the darkish hallway, they knew I was there.

Once again, I had to build up my bravery and strength and, using a kitchen chair, I climbed onto the windowsill. I scanned the area. There was nothing, so I slipped out of the window. I heard a ripping sound and I mentally screamed as my jogging bottoms caught on something, tearing the arse out of them. I now found myself bare arsed and hanging from a window. I was too butch and manly to cry, but it was a close call as I fought to be released. Why did everything have to be so hard?

Finally, I pulled myself clear and stumbled across the grit-covered concrete. There was a warm flush on both sets of my cheeks as the warm evening air wrapped itself around them. I was wearing the late

Mr Edwards' Nikes with the runner's sole. They gripped nicely and, almost silently, I made my way to the first car – a brand-new BMW. Don't ask me what model it was. All I knew was that it was silver. I peeked into the slightly tinted window.

'Shit,' I whispered when I saw that it was a stick shift, as the Americans call it. So that car was out. Next was a black Nissan. Swing and miss again. Another bloody manual.

I looked around hastily, checking the car park. The zombies were still all pressed up against the back door, searching for their evening meal. I kept my eyes on them as I ran to the final car, which seemed to be an older-style Honda CRV, and that's when things went wrong. My trainer caught a lone glass bottle, sending it flying into the said car, shattering the side window and making everything with a pair of ears turn towards the tinkling glass as it fell onto the concrete.

My eyes locked with the whitewashed eyes of the zombies. One by one, they turned and, in their usual lumbering gate, they headed towards me. I continued my journey towards the Honda CRV and slammed against the side.

'Yes!' I called out, although it didn't matter much as the meat eaters were on their way. I watched as they dragged their sun-rotted bodies towards me. I moved to the far side of the car so as to make an escape route towards the bedroom window – and, for once, my plan seemed to be working.

I started to run around the back of the car and then headed for the bedroom window, my bare arse flashing at the deadheads following me. The Nikes slipped a little, but I was nearly there. Then the horde started to pour around the corner like a zombie tsunami. It was going to be close.

'Come on, if Bruce Willis can do this shit, so can I,' I panted and threw myself through the open window. And that's when darkness took me over.

'Owww!' I groaned, but not as loudly as the zombies who were now trying to get through the window. I managed to retract my head and shoulder from the wardrobe. Thank God for cheap, flat-pack MDF, though my head did bloody hurt. The snapping of wood and the tearing of fabric echoed through the dark room as I fell against the bed. I was dizzy, but I needed to get out of the flat soon before those flesh eaters piled through the open window.

I crawled across the plush carpeting, pieces of cheap wood snagging onto my clothing and flesh as I tried to escape the mounds of putrefying flesh of the zombies that were trying to force their way through the opening. I stopped for a moment to admire their passion and drive to get their hands on me. What used to be human flesh was swollen from a lack of a good skincare regime and it burst, like overripe squashed tomatoes. It truly was a sight to behold. But the smell was beyond anything you could ever imagine.

I emptied my Weetabix-filled stomach onto the floor before continuing my journey, out into the fresh-smelling communal hallway.

It took me a while to get back onto my feet. The moans and groans of the not dead were still echoing through the building, despite the door of the flat being closed. This new world was starting to irk me somewhat. The first thing I had to do was pick the multitude of splinters from my baby-like skin – and that, I can tell you, took a while.

When the ache had dissipated, I gathered up all my supplies. The stash wasn't very impressive. I could survive on lager and toilet paper, as they were my most numerous items. But as long as I drank and shit myself, I would be okay.

I filled a rucksack I had found/stolen with toilet rolls, whatever water I had, and a few clothes. Anything else I needed I would have to scavenge along the way. I had five pairs of boxer shorts. And, as I was on my own, each one could last at least nearly a month – or more, if I turned them inside out. But not if they had buttons on the fly, as they would rip up Mr Happy, and I couldn't have that.

It was now night time and the flames were slowly engulfing the Cess Pool. I had to leave the next day. My plan was fluid – I would run out to the car and drive out of town as quickly as I could. Heading through town was out, and any route near a major city was also out. Since I was so close to London, going that way would mean death. This was where all those zombie films and books came in handy.

The sky was aglow with flames licking at the stars. I had taken my rucksack, plus another bottle of water, to the late Mr Edwards' flat so that I could use his ground-floor window, which happened to be zombie free, to get to the car. I would then go, all fast and furious, and get out of this bloody town and into the countryside. I would then hopefully meet up with survivors, who wouldn't rape or kill me and use my skin as a blanket. I knew there were several large farms as well as a scattering of smallholdings that I could hold up in for a while. I wondered if there was a cow that shat Pringles?

I slept fitfully that night. The zombies were getting agitated by the oncoming firestorm. I had heard a few screams in the night from people being forced out of hiding and into the teeth of death from bites, or flames. Either way, they ended their days in unbridled pain.

The sun was nearly up. It was time to go. I did my last check and picked up a photo of my late parents, as well as the secret one of Olga and me when she gave me a kiss on my birthday. I had tried to give her a kiss on her birthday, but that, my friends, didn't go as well. That girl could certainly pack a punch.

The window opened almost silently; all the zombies were still trying to force themselves into the other open window. I lowered my bag out of the flat and dropped it onto the concrete as quietly as I could. Luckily, the deadheads were making a racket, which allowed me to drop to the ground like a motherfucking ninja... again, but I did refrain from doing any Bruce Lee sound effects. I retrieved my bottle of water, then slowly closed the window. There was always the chance I would have to come back – if the building hadn't burnt down in the meantime.

Crouched over, I ran over to the Honda, making sure there were no glass footballs in my way this time. I hid by the driver's door, ensuring I was out of sight of the window-loving walkers. My breathing was heavy – not out of tiredness or lack of exercise, but out of sheer panic. I clicked the key fob and heard the door locks disengage. I took a quick look at the zombies, but they hadn't reacted at all. They just carried on their game of hide and seek.

The driver's door opened with a click and a creak, not nearly as loud as my train-wreck of an imagination told me it would be. I manhandled my bag across the driver's seat and into the passenger seat and threw the water into the footwell, which made a soft thud. The noise didn't travel, however. It looked like the god of good luck was with me for the time being.

I eased into the driver's seat and closed the door with a soft click. It didn't look closed completely, but it would do for now. The zombies hadn't noticed a thing so far. I took in the many controls and my mind started to close. There were so many of them. Pedal right to go and left to stop. No clutch, wooohooo! Gearstick with a button on the side, which you press in to move it to D for drive. That taxi ride home had come in handy before the world went to shit.

Then there was the handbrake. Like the gear selector, it had a button to press to allow you to take it off. It sounded so easy in my head. I looked at the route ahead; it was a straight drive past the flat, turn left, then down the hill, and then just go where it was clear. I put the key in the ignition. I turned it a couple of clicks and the dashboard came alight like New Year's Eve. Then came the beeps of alarm that started to annoy me; but, once again, the beep to zombie moan ratio was still positive for me.

I turned the key. It didn't catch straight away, but it made negative things happen. The flesh eaters were beginning to stop their onslaught against the window; some of them had their facial tissue sheared of by the pressure of their brothers and sisters as a result of ramming their faces against the sharp-edged PVC window frame. The sight alone made me bulk. I was dragged from the visual hell by the sound of the engine finally catching.

'SWEEEEET!' I looked around and noticed that the car had a dock for my iPod. But the sight of more walkers coming towards the car focused my mind onto more important things, for now.

'WHY WON'T YOU FUCKING WORK?' The gearstick wouldn't move. I revved the engine. I had a full tank of petrol. The button on the side of the gear selector was pressed. 'Okay... parking brake off... Done. Put in drive...' I almost screamed as the selector refused to budge.

The car jumped as the first deadhead hit the front of the car and the fear in me started to rouse. I just didn't know what I was doing. The horde was gathering in numbers. I slammed my foot onto the brake and, like the divine touch from the heavens, the gear selector went all the way down with a thump.

'Yeah, bitch!' I moved it back up to drive and slowly pressed the accelerator, making the revs build. It was the sheer number of the dead that was now stopping my escape. My breathing became rapid and sweat poured into my eyes.

'EAT SHIT!' I slammed my foot onto the accelerator, forcing me back into the leather chair and sending the revs into the red, turning the vehicle into a weapon as it flew forwards.

BEEP!!

'Ow! What the fuck…' I muttered, my vision wavering. I could hear the engine still running. The air bag had exploded into my face. No wonder my bloody face was hurting.

The horn finally stopped. I deflated the airbag using the multi tool that I'd found in one of the flats. How's that for forward thinking? In the Mirrors I could see the zombies that had survived my attempted escape, slowly making their way towards me.

All those years playing Grand Theft Auto had obviously done nothing for me. I managed to get the car into reverse and moved away from the Mini I had just destroyed, but I had made a good choice on cars, as this bad boy was still running okay. I noticed more walkers coming up the hill from the town, either as a result of the noise I'd made or were fleeing the fire. So I managed to slowly push through the sun-damaged zombies and headed up the hill and away from my stalkers.

The roads were littered with rotting bodies and burnt-out cars. I had certainly slept through an apocalypse. I would have to think up a good lie for when I got asked, 'Where were you when the Zombie Apocalypse started?' I don't think 'Blitzed out of my head on Viagra and Red Bull' would impress people.

My driving skills were crap, and my attention span even worse – especially as I had finally put my iPod through the stereo, which allowed it to charge up, too. I know Culture Club isn't the most popular road trip music ever, but it calmed me. It had taken me three hours to finally reach open country – which was lucky, as steam had started to leak from the Honda's slightly bent bonnet.

I pulled over and stared at the instrument display. The fuel was lowish, but another thing was very high – it had a picture of a thermometer. I knew that couldn't be good. *Oh, my aching face...* I began to realise that my crash into the Mini had done more damage than I had at first thought. Normally in films, when an engine is overheating they either fill the radiator with water or replace the fan belt with a lady's stocking.

Getting out of the car, I decided to make my way on foot. My backpack felt heavy on my back as I started off to a house I could see in the distance. The weather was mild, but my back was coated in sweat as I walked down the road, leaving the car still steaming. Twenty minutes later, I was panting. Clearly, my cardio workout regime was somewhat lacking. I climbed over a five-bar metal gate and began to cross over an empty field towards the back of the large, brick house. Unfortunately, I could see way too many fields littered with the corpses of animals that were now carrion for the birds and foxes.

From my view of the back garden, I could see no movement in the grounds or the house itself. It was a two-storey house with a large lawn that had seen better days. Luckily, it had access to the field that surrounded the property via a wrought iron kissing gate. I moved like a well-trained Special Forces operator, making no sound, until my backpack caught the gate and sent it slamming into the metal surround, which seemed to reverberate through the quiet countryside. But still no zombie sounds.

I kept to the edge of the lawn, keeping my eyes on the property and my back to the surrounding hedge. There was still no movement in or around the house. I did see a small greenhouse, but I speculated that anything worth eating would have wilted in the English summer. As I passed the dirtied window, I could see that I was right; a rotten mash of tomatoes lay piled on the dirt floor.

'What a waste,' I said to myself and continued on my journey.

I made a circuit of the house, passing a garden shed and a standalone garage, which would need looking into soon. The property showed no sign of life. There were no cars in the drive, no chickens in the yard – well, that's what people in the country have, I presumed. All the doors were locked. I made my way back to the garden and there lay a watering can by a hosepipe. Once again, the goddess of luck had touched me. As the water flowed, I stretched my back out with relief, having crept all this way hunched over. After a few minutes, I took in a deep breath. There was a strange smell in the air, almost like burning plastic, or something like that.

The plan was to leave the bag, fill the watering can with water and replenish the water tank in the car, then hopefully kip here for the night. It showed no signs of zombie infestation. I just had to break in without doing too much damage. I also needed a place to live, as the last embers of the summer were floating by quickly and soon the rain would come. I needed a base that had food and water. That thought made me chuckle.

'How about a waitress from Hooters, too?' I said and turned off the water tap, having now filled the watering can. I sniffed. 'What *is* that stink?'

I dropped my backpack and took a lingering drink from the dwindling supply of water and headed back down the shingle driveway – a good thing, as I would always hear people and cars coming up the narrow and long driveway. The drive was walled in by the once well-tended hedges; now, however, any vehicle that would try and get here would have many a micro scratch before they got to the house.

As I continued cautiously down the drive, I reached a heavy wooden bar gate, which opened on oiled hinges. Being the horror movie that my life had now become, I had expected the gate to creak loudly, shouting to all flesh eaters, '*Chubby man who can't run here, eat your fill.*' But, it didn't, so I slowly moved off in the direction of my car and the strange smell. Clearly, something was on fire as there was now a trail of smoke being spread across the sky by gusts of wind.

'Right…' I said and stopped dead when I saw the cause of the smoke and smell. The watering can fell from my hand, instantly wetting my trousers. It was no longer needed, as I watched my means of escape burning and melting. Something important had obviously gone *boom!* in the car, and at that moment something did send me to the ground, as a wing mirror of death shot past, nearly taking my head off. I swear to this day that I could see the look of panic reflected in the mirror as it passed me.

The flames that were licking at the fluffy white clouds were at least helping to dry my trousers as my still prone body sobbed violently. No, I wasn't crying; my eyes were producing water to help cool down my hot cheeks, and that's the story I am sticking to. So that laughing squirrel can piss off.

Chapter 5

Unknown place and time - I wasn't paying attention

I made it back to the house, dragging the now empty green watering can along with me, just in case I decided to fill it up with my tears. I locked the gate behind me and, apart from a bramble tearing at my shirt, I made it to the house unscathed and celebrated the fact by throwing the plastic receptacle down in disgust. This wasn't the way things were meant to go. Who'd have thought that surviving a zombie apocalypse would be so hard? I washed my face using the outside tap and stared up into the big sky. Not a single plane could be seen. Perhaps I was not actually conscious? Maybe I was in hospital, linked up to lots of machines that go 'bing' after stroking out following my Red Bull and Viagra combo? Not the best move I had ever made, that one.

There were darkening clouds on the horizon and a summer rainstorm heading my way. I could almost smell the rain coming to cleanse the earth again. I had to act, so I checked the front door. It was large and bright red, but it was locked very securely.

'Untrusting bastard,' I said and kicked it, feeling something crack in my foot. Hopefully, it was just a toenail.

I limped around the side of the building. There was a kitchen door – a stable door, the type where the top can open independently. But not this time, as both parts were locked solid. So much for the friendly and welcoming country folk. They had some major trust issues. I went around to the back again, which was mainly windows with large ornate patio doors – large, ornate and very locked patio doors, at that. Yes, I could smash them, but that would leave me a tad exposed when the hedgehog revolution came about. Don't laugh – it's coming, people. They are the silent killers.

As the light started to dip thanks to the oncoming clouds, I took a minute to think. Smashing anything big would be a bad idea, even for me. My foot was back to normal now, so at least I didn't have to do the zombie shuffle as I chose my entry point. The wind was starting to pick up, throwing debris around. I saw large, orange Propane tanks by the kitchen in a wire mesh cage. I deduced from this that the residents weren't on the gas mains. I hoped that the tanks were full, but that would be a job for later.

Just past the kitchen was a frosted window at my head height. It was big enough for me to climb through, and was hopefully just a storage cupboard, or a possible bathroom. But how to get up there? And here comes the A-team montage. If only.

I dragged a metal garden bench up to the wall. By standing on it, this now put me at shoulder height to the window. I *deemed* that it was not high enough. That word-a-day calendar at home really had improved my language skills. I found a pile of old house bricks by the greenhouse and I piled them onto the bench, enough so that both feet had a good base to stand on. Yes, it was a bit shaky, but I had faith. Climbing up, I then lofted up one of the bricks and smashed the glass.

'FUCK YOU, GLASS!' Take that, Noel Coward. I was now covered in blood, brick dust and glass. The brick disintegrated in my hand, but it did breach the window.

The blood flowed onto the driveway as I held the cut under the outside tap. Clearly, my future as a cat burglar was in jeopardy. It was then that I realised I could see into the future, as I saw myself getting soaked. My prediction was about to come true as the heavens opened and the English summer disappeared. It was always just a fleeting friend.

I trotted back around to where the semi-broken window still mocked me. I chose another brick and freed the frame of any residual glass that could force me to swap genders quickly and messily. And yes, it was a bathroom, consisting of a simple toilet with a small sink. As the rain thumped on to my head, I began my entrance into the house. Unfortunately, I went in headfirst, hoping I could find some purchase inside to allow me to turn around and drop gracefully onto the tiled floor.

'Fuuuccckkk!!'

Now, how to describe my position in said room? Okay, I am in pain. Body versus porcelain; you will always lose that battle, my friend. At this moment in time, my face was on the tiled floor with my right arm for company. My left arm was behind me and it was wet with what, I assumed to be, blood, though my thoughts then leant towards toilet water. The rest of my bruised and battered body was resting against the wall, underneath the window, with my legs waving about trying to find purchase. After acknowledging my position and knowing that there was never going to be a pain-free or graceful way of getting out of there, let's just say I did.

To describe how I managed to get out of said position in the small bathroom would take a long, convoluted description and possibly void my man card. I know men should show emotion and cry, but this is not the time or place for me to tell you that. So, after a feat of impressive gymnastics and yoga moves that would make a new-age man hard, I walked out of that little prison not with a swagger but a slight limp.

Unconcerned for my own safety, but not checking the property out first, I tried and failed to open the front door to reclaim my bag as the main dead lock needed a key. So back to the kitchen I went, out of the kitchen door and straight into the storm. The rain was driving sideways, absolutely soaking me as I dashed to the front, grabbed my bag and headed back into the house. Just then, the good Lord himself turned the tap off. That's just the way summer storms play out.

I sat at the pine kitchen table and took in my surroundings. It was pine heaven – but not the cheap kind. It was all solid wood. I crossed my arms on the cool wood and put my head down onto it, letting the exhaustion flow over me and drag me into slumber. I hoped the dreams wouldn't come – well, they did, but they were of Olga, who willingly wore the maid's outfit I had bought her. But then there were other flashes of her smiling and chiding me at times. I did miss her brisk chats about her times growing up in Russia.

When I awoke, the sun was failing in the sky. I walked around the large house, inspecting the four bedrooms, dining room, and what seemed to be a boot room full of waterproof jackets and wellington boots. There was some post on a French polished table by the front door. Colonel Arnold Sebastian Hargreaves. No wonder the place was so well kept and organised.

I found some candles in the kitchen as, like everywhere else, there was no electric. But I did find some Kettle chips and a bottle of lemonade, so I ate and drank as I wandered around the house until I fell, fully clothed, onto a bed in one of the spare rooms, my bag and a freshly refilled bottle of water by my side. If I survived the night, I would see what this house would hold for me.

The sun cast a pattern across the white-painted bedroom. As beautiful as it looked, the rays penetrated my brain and dragged me into consciousness.

'Ah, fuck!' I muttered and dragged my lazy, smelly arse off the bed. As in my workdays, I sat on the side of the bed and placed my face in my hands, this time just to gather my thoughts for the day.

Managing to stand up, I walked from room to room, the plush carpeting absorbing my footsteps. However, being cream coloured it showed exactly the route I had taken with my dirty shoes. I checked every window and saw nothing. Even the garden gate was still closed, which was a good sign – or else the walking dead had become more considerate and closed it behind them. I hate my mind!

I AM CLEAN. The power shower obviously didn't work – as stated in the name, it required power to cover my dirty body with steaming hot water. So, I had a cold bath and, yes, the parts that designated me as a male retracted and hid inside me somewhere, but it was still good to feel clean again. Afterwards, I walked around in a fluffy white towelling robe with matching slippers.

The house was a truly creepy place, so quiet and old with sash windows, but with up-to-date electronics and furniture. If only I could get some power.

I took a pad of lined paper and a pen, which I found next to the dead phone, to be used for the making of lists – which, unless this was just a local zombie apocalypse and the phones would come back online, would never be used to take messages from Aunt Margaret again. Saying localised aloud didn't quite sound right. Could you have a localised apocalypse?

However, if this was just a UK thing, the Yanks would swoop in and save the day with their Apache helicopters and Burger Kings. I could do with a Whopper right now. A tear ran down my cheek, knowing that I would never again get to sink my teeth into one. I know it's bullshit, but a man can dream. Blame Hollywood.

My dreaming came to an end when, in my musing, I opened the fridge. The splatter of vomit hit the stone flagged flooring, coating my slippers and shins with last night's Kettle crisps, and I slammed the door of the fridge closed. That was now one of the rules of the new world – leave fridges alone. Anything in there would be ruined and anything that could've survived just wasn't worth it.

I stripped off and found some black bin bags, using the robe to clean up the mess. Then, with the help of some cleaning products from under the sink, the kitchen began to smell better. Everything was placed into the back bags. After cleaning up, I discovered that the two halves of the kitchen door were bolted together, which was quickly remedied. I opened the top half of the stable kitchen door and launched the rubbish out, into the morning sun.

The bath water was still there from last night. Yes, it was a bit funky, but waste not want not, so I added some shower gel to freshen it up and had a quick dunk. I used the pink towel to dry my bits (thank you, Mrs Hargreaves). I needed to act smart. In all the films I had seen, it was the lazy ones who had been killed. So I dressed and put on the Colonel's walking boots – they were a bit big, but they would do the job. Then I placed my bag on the kitchen table, just in case I had to flee, as the kitchen door was the only exit.

Picking up the note pad and pen, I started to write out a plan for the day:

Check for foods

Check gas outside

Find out what the bloody date is

Check every cupboard and drawer for anything of use

Check for porn

Search out buildings.

It seemed that the lady of the house kept her cupboards well stocked. Clearly, this was a summer house as it was all cans, dried pastas, jars of homemade pasta sauce, and bags of rice. The holy grail was the larder; it looked like she had bought all the homemade marmalades and jams in the county. The potatoes had all gone feral, but I might plant them in the garden and see what happens. If Matt Damon can do that on the planet Mars, then why can't I? Maybe in the greenhouse? It all depended when you were meant to plant the bloody things.

But, by the looks of things, I could survive the winter if I decided to. I popped outside carrying a wicked machete that I had found in the larder. *Rhubarb must be quite vicious in this part of the country*, I thought and chuckled at my own wit.

Of the two Propane bottles, one was full, the other was only half full. See what I did there? A negative person would say half empty. Up yours, doubters. I just had to find out what it was used for. The kitchen was a good size. The hob was gas, but the oven was electric, which meant that at least I could boil things if the water held out. There were about six two-litre bottles of water in the larder, but I would have to conserve those for drinking and just in case I might have to leave.

Feeling proud of myself, I kicked into self-survival mode. I inspected the garden shed, which turned out to be disappointing as it held a mower, shovel, spade, and general garden tools. No machine guns, or materials for making a tank. So no apocalypse warrior for me, then. The good thing about the shed was that the guttering fed into a waist-high plastic water barrel – and, thank the gods of the Zombie Apocalypse, it was all new, so I could see all the way down to the bottom. Perfect for using for boiling and filling the toilet cistern once the English summer reverts to is normal state of continuous rain. So, I managed to find something to cover the top of the barrel to protect it from any suicidal pigeons, or those who had found religion and had decided to try their wings at avian baptism.

I ran inside, grabbed a small pan, filled it three quarters full and put it onto the hob to boil. Within five minutes I had a steaming hot cup of black tea and a couple of chocolate biscuits that were fresh out of the packet. For the first time in a while, I felt safe and happy. Yes, my body still hurt from having fallen through the window and hitting what felt like a porcelain hammer, but the cold baths had soothed my aching muscles and bones.

After using the downstairs toilet, which was a bit messy due to my breaking the window, I added to my list *fix the bloody window, and leave toilet rolls in sun to dry out*. Toilet rolls were like gold dust nowadays.

I decided the shitter window was the first item to fix, the rest could wait. The Colonel or his wife were fans of labelling things, so I went to the key rack and saw a couple of keys tied together by a piece of white string with a brown label showing the word Garage in black ink written on it. I grabbed the keys off the hook and headed out, after making sure there wasn't a key labelled Tank or Car (unfortunately, there wasn't).

The side door on the garage unlocked, but it took all my strength to yank the door open. Then I could see why. The door was an old, wooden one and it had warped in its frame, most probably from the rain and heat. After my Herculean effort, I stepped into the dark recesses of the garage, and possibly to my death. What kind of idiot was I? Maybe I should wear a blonde wig and ask, 'Hello, is anybody there?'

I stepped back out into the morning light and took a flashlight that I had found in one of the kitchen drawers. The fact that it worked helped as I entered the dark garage once more, with the torch in one hand and the machete in the other, its blade gleaming in the torchlight. The garage was empty, as I had guessed, of cars and the undead. So, after making sure I wasn't about to be feasted upon, I took the keys to the double wooden doors at the front of the garage. These opened a lot easier than the warped side door, and it bathed the garage in daylight. There were tools hanging off the wall in regimental fashion – you could tell the Colonel was an Army man, through and through.

I'm not a fan of DIY or any kind of manual labour, but a man must do what a man must do – though, as I couldn't phone a handyman, I would have to strive to do it myself. I tried to think about all the DIY programmes I had watched during my life on a sofa.

That came to nothing, so I opened a couple of drawers from a large wooden work bench. And there it was – a tape measure. I took that out, collected the note pad and pen from the kitchen, made my way outside and stared up at the broken window.

The bench was still there so I restacked the bricks, making it feel a bit more secure, and climbed up and took the dimensions. I remembered a saying that I had heard once – measure twice, cut once. Maybe that's for later. The bricks shifted slightly as I moved. Amazingly, the house still had wooden window frames, so hopefully I could hammer something against the frame to block up the hole.

I dropped down, hearing the sound of either my ankles or knees cracking painfully, making me swear once more. I limped to the garage and began to search for something that I wouldn't have to alter too much, knowing I wasn't very skilled with a blade.

Cardboard? Nope. Glass? Nope – if I could get a nail through that I would be named magician of the year. I looked through the garage and found something that might do – if I remembered rightly, it was called plasterboard (or, in the good old USA, drywall). It was larger than I needed – but hey, Mr DIY here we come. I placed the slab on the work bench and measured out the dimensions I needed, but now I needed something to cut it with.

'Victory!' I called out into the lonely heavens and picked up the saw, readying myself to make the first cut (Dad would be so proud).

'FUCK! WANK!' The saw destroyed it, ripping it to shit. All the chalky plaster stuff in the middle fell into lumps or dust.

I stood back and brushed all the crap off my jeans and trainers and looked around the bench. I had ruined only part of the board, so I remeasured and drew the lines using a piece of wood to make sure the line would be straight. I held the wood in place and picked up a sharp, cutting tool with a small triangle blade and dug it into the plaster, dragging it down the wood's edge, cutting deep into the board. It took a few goes before the tip of the blade dug into the work bench. I closed my eyes and smiled. Finally, something was going my way. And so, with a smile on my face, I continued to finish my own personal Sistine Chapel.

'Eat dick, Michelangelo,' I mocked.

Before taking my victory lap, I found some nails and a nice hammer. I carried out all my equipment and walked back to the window. Climbing up on the bricks, my footing shifted, but I was still safe. So, with trumpets of celebration in my ears, I placed the board against the hole that was once the window. And then I watched as it fell straight through, smashing itself onto the porcelain throne below.

If somebody were to have walked past right then, they might have seen me sitting on the bench with my face in my hands, a plethora of curse words flying from my mouth and tears of anger rolling down my cheek. Instead, however, they would see a man who was merely contemplating life and being overcome with emotion. However, the realisation that I had measured the space where the glass had once sat and not the frame itself was too much. It's times like these that I am happy to be alone. At this rate, I wouldn't even impress a toddler with my DIY skills.

After another two hours of work, I'm man enough to admit some tears, but the job was finished. However, before nailing it to the frame I wrapped it with some plastic sheeting from the garage so that, when the winter hit, the toilet would stay fairly dry.

It had amazed me how long such an easy-looking job had taken, even with my skill set. I began to feel weak and I realised I must have been a tad dehydrated from the sweat and manly tears. So, using water from the barrel outside, and after putting it through the water filter that I found in the fridge – yes, I braved it once more – I boiled up some pasta and a little of the homemade sauce. It was divine and, with a glass of red wine in my hand, I ate alone and enjoyed watching the birds fluttering to their roost as the sun came down. I knew that tomorrow I would have to search this house top to bottom.

Chapter 6

TIME/DATE/PLACE… DON'T KNOW, DON'T CARE

Day two in the Hargreaves house

I will be the first to admit that I am a lazy arse, and the local wildlife had been telling me so, for hours. It was my last wash in the tub as the water was starting to look more than a bit third hand. So, away down the plughole it went. I washed the tub out quickly and then refilled it, hoping the water would still last. And it did, this time.

My daily checks involved making sure the grounds were devoid of the walking dead. Luckily, the fences and the big front gate had kept all those whose life had left them, away. It was all clear, so I headed back inside for a small breakfast and COFFFEEE!

I began my search of the house, starting with the lounge. I checked all the drawers and cupboards, and anything deemed of use I left in plain sight. While I did that, I put away all the ghostly family pictures. It was spooky having all those faces staring at me while I defiled their lovely home.

The door in the kitchen that I thought was just another storage cupboard turned out to be an access to the cellar, and that's where I found it – boxes of Christmas decorations and general crap. Not only that, but I would always have wine to drink, as there were at least a hundred bottles of wine placed in a rustic-looking iron wine rack. The room itself was not very useful, except for using it as a hidey hole should I be invaded by the man munchers. However, being a basement, the downside was that I would be trapped.

I had been through most of the downstairs rooms now. The last one was the Colonel's study, which was adorned with pictures from his army days. He had obviously been through all the major engagements, including Northern Ireland, the Falklands to sand dancing with the Iraqis and Afghans. There were books on the army and biographies of generals and political leaders. He loved what he did, by the looks of it.

'Oh… my… God!' I said loudly as I pulled out a handgun from inside the Colonel's desk drawer. Trying to keep a check on my excitement, I held the gun in my right hand and lovingly stroked it like any man would. It seemed to be a World War II German Luger. I remembered from my Call of Duty sessions, and some TV documentaries, how it worked. So, with my thumb and forefinger, I pulled back the what I will call the 'charging handle', which normally allows you to see if there are any bullets in the breech or the magazine. Yep, I know my shit.

After finding the gun empty, I worked out how to release the magazine that was situated inside the handle. Now the search was on for bullets, which would allow me a certain amount of safety, from dead and alive.

'SCORE!' I jumped up and did a little jig as a box of fifty 9 mm bullets appeared from the back of the drawer. Feeling as excited as a kid at Christmas, I loaded the magazine, slammed it home and, once again, pulled back the charging handle. The brass casing of the bullet slid deftly into the breech, ready to be fired. I clicked on the safety catch and placed it back onto the desk to continue my search.

There was nothing else of note in the study. So, while carrying the now deadly weapon like a first born, I headed upstairs, leaving the bullets on the desk. The stairs creaked as I ascended and I began the long search of the first-floor rooms. Mr Hargreaves' clothes were thrown onto the bed, along with underwear and socks. I couldn't be proud at this moment in time, as it had been a long while since I'd worn my own underwear, may they rest in peace. And, although I would now have to wear an old man's pants, on my grave, I would never wear his wife's knickers… unless I really had to, but I did steal her socks.

His clothes were a few sizes too large for me; however, with a belt the trousers would stay up, and the rest didn't matter. The other rooms were fairly bare, until I reached the smallest room in the house. This room only had a small, single bed with a rickety-looking bedside table, which was painted white to match the rest of the room. Bloody thing looked like a clean room. I opened the cupboard in the corner and there it stood, like the star over a stable in Bethlehem.

It was a metal cabinet, tall and thin, no more than a foot wide. Above it sat a curled, leather belt full of shotgun cartridges. They were all red in colour, which didn't mean anything to me, but the belt was full – twenty-three cartridges, to be precise. I threw it on the bed, which made my pistol bounce up in the air, scaring me slightly. I had to be careful with these things. This was real life, after all.

I checked every key in the house, but all my careful searching was for nought. The master of the house was always a careful one and must have carried it with him. The git. I carried my little death bringer outside – and I won't lie, I did aim at things and go BANG. But I was careful and checked the boundaries of the property. I was hoping for a shotgun which would allow me to at least shoot some fresh food and maybe take vengeance upon that laughing squirrel. Not that I knew how to shoot or prepare the food, but we all must start somewhere. Hopefully, I would come across a sitting rabbit or a pheasant that would have a heart attack while I walked past it – and, if it could clean itself too, that would be just super.

Walking into the garage, I looked at the row of tools. 'Right, you buggers. Which of you will open it up?'

There was a toolbox that I took, along with a couple of larger hammers. I put my gun in my front pocket, giving me a bulge to impress the ladies, had there been any about. I dragged the tools up the stairs and, with every step, the toolbox banged against either the wall or the stairs. I imagined the gun firing and the bullet effeminising me. A cold shiver made me walk more carefully.

I placed the unhygienic castration machine on the white bedside table in the tiny bedroom and placed all the tools I had brought upstairs on the bed. There were a whole assortment of hammers, from small to a big 'fuck you' one, screwdrivers, and, if I remember rightly from school, some chisels. But as the cabinet was metal and not wood, they might not be needed, and I stress might!

First was a screwdriver into the keyhole and, with the help of a medium-sized hammer, I hoped it would easily destroy the lock. I placed the tool into the hole and lined up the hammer with the top of the said screwdriver, and gave it a few tentative taps, then a heavy hit. BANG. Nope. BANG. Nope. Okay, a harder hit, this time.

'One, two, three…' BANG. 'ARGHHH!! MOTHERFUCKINGHATEFULPIECEOFSHIT!' I screamed and fell to the floor, dropping my hammer, leaving the screwdriver that I had partially missed hanging from the lock mockingly. I cradled my throbbing hand, which had now lost some skin from several fingers.

Two hours later, a husk of a man sat on a ruined carpet, with a screwdriver that was now covered in the man's blood and tears. The door to the cupboard was hanging by the top hinge only. Tools littered the once prestige room; the Colonel would be most upset.

The gun safe still looked like a safe; it was just scratched like a cat's scratching post. I truly didn't know what to do now. If this was a comedy, the door would open on its own with a comical creak. I guess they made it this way to stop people like me stealing firearms and harming innocents.

I dragged my sorry self downstairs and opened a bottle of wine. I was alone, hopeless, and nothing was going to change that anytime soon. My vision blurred as I stared out the French doors at the back of the house. Tears ran rivers down my cheeks and didn't stop even when the wine had run out and darkness claimed the land as its own. I needed to grow up.

The next day broke, my body warmed by the sun's rays filtering through the same door that had witnessed me at my lowest point yet. I peeled my drool and tear-covered face off the lounge carpet – there must have been an earthquake in the night that had thrown me off the sofa. My head pounded with the after effects of the wine.

Luckily, the woman of the house had plenty of headache tablets, which allowed me to function like a human lookalike by midday. I could then begin my checks as I had done the day before. Today was different, though, as there was a noise coming from down the road. It sounded like it was being driven to me via the wind, and it wasn't man-made like a car or motorbike. It was a sound I had never heard before, but it was coming my way.

The front gate was secured with a latch, but that was all, so I made my way out to the garage and searched as quickly as I could. Within twenty minutes, I'd found a hefty chain and, in a drawer, a large padlock with a key still in it. At last, something was going my way. So, moving quickly – well, as much as my head would allow – I managed to chain the gate securely, so that anything that was coming this way would have a difficult time of it.

I made sure I had plenty of boiled water, just in case I couldn't leave the house for a while, and then kept watch up in the front bedroom. Periodically, I did go back to the safe and hit it with a lump hammer – it didn't open it, but it made me feel better.

The noise from outside had been continuing for some hours now and had started to vibrate the window. A trail of dust was being kicked up by the same thing that was heading this way. I could only imagine that it was a zombie horde. Just like in the films, they decimate towns and cities, then just walk on, consuming any living human beings that dare show themselves.

The evening came and I continued to watch from the front bedroom window all night. The noise was building – a constant groaning sound, like a depressed behemoth.

Something inside me was telling me to run, or at least head into the fields that surrounded the house. And that voice had grown even louder as the sun crept up over the horizon the next morning. And then I saw them – a constant stream of zombies shuffling past the gateway to the house. I was glad I had locked it with that chain, especially as it was flexing as the bodies bounced against it in their erratic pace. But then something happened – a zombie girl hit the gate and was turned around to face the house by the rebound off her fellow corpses. Then she stared up the driveway as if she was searching for life. From her attire, I guessed she had been at the gym when she turned.

A brief interlude

The story of Zoe the Zombie

'Get some KFC after, Zoe!'

Zoe Williams rolled her eyes as she slid her new Apple phone into her gym bag.

'Mum, I'm going to the gym. I need to get myself ready for my holiday, not a takeaway run,' she said and checked her make-up in the hallway mirror, just in case Justin the personal trainer would be there. He was fit as fuck, after all.

The kitchen door opened. 'Oh, please, love,' said her mother, Angela. 'Your father and brother are out at the Wanderers tonight [local football team], and I can't be bothered to cook. Be a good girl and get you mum some finger licking.' She gave a filthy laugh as she licked at her badly painted nails.

'Yuck, you filthy bitch,' Zoe shot back. But she knew her mother would have her own way. The girl had planned to eat a few pieces of chicken after the gym, anyway. Why else would they build a gym on top of a chicken restaurant? 'Fine, but you'll have to wait, all right?' she added, slinging her bag over her shoulder.

Her bleached-blonde mother smiled. 'Ah, thanks, luv. Enjoy your workout, and say hi to that Justin from me.' She chuckled and ran off screaming as a phonebook was thrown at her. It missed its aim, slamming into the kitchen door.

The 29-year-old unemployed hairdresser shook her head and grabbed her car keys, hoping her Ford Focus would start. She slammed the front door closed and bounced away to her car. Her new trainers were whiter than virginal snow and set her look off perfectly. The car did start, so tonight was going to be her night.

Zoe drove off into town, heading for the business park. It didn't take long – to be honest, it took her longer to find a parking space.

'Come on, twat!' she screamed at a confused old person in a Jaguar. 'For fuck's sake…' She finally made it to a space. With one last check in the mirror, just in case the muscled god was here, she got out of the car.

She walked into the room of pain and sweat, only to see it mostly empty. All the staff were gathered around the TV on the wall. Zoe squinted.

'Sky news? Where's MTV?' she muttered to herself, looking around and noting that Justin wasn't about. By the looks of it, she would spend more time eating chicken than chatting up a hunky man that evening. She huffed and walked to the changing room.

The tall brunette tightened her ponytail, allowing her hair to fall between her shoulder blades, and headed to the treadmill. She was even wearing a new sports bra and top to give Justin a bit of a show, but the only man to have the show was the soon-to-be heart attack victim on the rowing machine, who was now a very fetching colour of red and purple blotches.

Stepping on the treadmill, Zoe began to slowly build up speed on the machine, when she noticed something was wrong. She caught a glimpse of the staff running out of the door. They had left the till open, too. They must have decided to rob the place.

'Kids!' she scoffed and slowed down the machine to walking pace, then stopped.

She was barely out of breath. That's why she noticed the lack of noise. Zoe knew she had been left alone. *Sod this*, she thought, running off to collect her things.

And that is what ended her life – that, and stopping to check her make-up before leaving the changing room. She calmed herself and walked out, heading to the stairs.

A growling noise came from the bottom of the stairs. Zoe stopped dead. It sounded like a bloody dog.

'Hello?' she said, and then rolled her eyes at what she had just said. How many horror films had she and her friend, Hannah, seen? They always mocked the blonde with the big false tits who said such a thing before being murdered.

She heard footsteps on the stairs, but they were uncoordinated. Zoe looked around and found a small, pink dumbbell on the floor. It would be easier to swing and make the groaning twat think twice.

Her breathing quickened as the sound of footsteps came up the stairs. Then, a shaven-headed man turned the corner. He was toned, but bloodied. It was her personal trainer. She sighed with relief.

'Justin, thank God!' Zoe called out with a little jump, trying to show off her new trainers.

Her smile faltered as the man turned towards her. Half of Justin's cheek was gone. Zoe could see his perfect teeth that were admired by all the girls, and some boys, at the sweat club. Part of her wanted to see if he was okay, hug him and press his face to her chest and say, 'There, there, Zoe is here.' But the larger part of her just wanted to run. Something was wrong with him.

As she stared at the man who was once Justin Matthews, he ran at her and bowled her over. As they both went down, the pink dumbbell came up and slammed into his perfect white teeth, making some of them take flight. Panic rose as she fought against the man. His breath smelt like a bin, and he kept on biting the air.

'YOU'RE A FUCKING ZOMBIE!' she screamed. In a moment of sheer panic, she slammed the dumbbell into the side of the man's head. She then twisted her body and managed to get his stinking weight off her.

Zoe scrabbled up onto her new trainers and tried to tun.

'OWWW!' she screamed, feeling pain flooding through her body. She turned and saw the man she had once fancied biting into her calf, spoiling her trainers. She screamed again in agony. Using her other trainer, she tried to kick him off. It worked. But, just like in the movies, she was buggered. She stood up and leant against one of the exercise machines as the zombie fought to reclaim its footing.

Zoe's eyes flitted about and saw a bigger dumbbell, but she couldn't lift it. By the time she found one that she could, Justin was on his way, albeit slowly. She waited until he'd got closer, then with all her strength she hit him on the jaw, dislocating it fully, and making him groan even more. The next hit sent him to the ground and, while screaming blue murder, she turned his head into a bloody pulp.

Zoe Williams sat on the cheap, carpeted floor and cried. She cried for Justin, the mother she would never see again, and the life that was going to end. She knew this as her stomach was turning itself inside out and dark veins were shooting from her calf wound, which was no longer bleeding. Her vision became blurred and then her head swam. She tried to think about things, but it was like catching smoke. The last thought the ex-hairdresser had as she died, sitting looking herself in the mirrored wall opposite, was how good she looked, and that she hoped her mum and family were okay.

As Zoe passed into darkness, her family members were already waiting to meet her on the other side. Five minutes after she'd left her house that evening, a neighbour had popped around after having been bitten by her husband. When the woman turned, Angela Williams was torn to pieces by her friend. And, thanks to the granite kitchen top that her head hit on its way down, she wouldn't walk again, unlike the rest of her family. The men of the house were lost as soon as they became infected, and turned while watching the football. The full capacity crowd had nowhere to go; they would spend the rest of their undead lives staring at a field of overgrown grass with zombies in colourful jerseys shuffling about.

Zoe the Zombie woke up, her cloudy eyes staring at herself in the mirror. Though the person opposite looked very pretty, she didn't realise it was her own reflection. She was suddenly aware that she could sense fresh food. She stood up and headed outside, with only one thought – to feed and sate the burning in her core. So that's what she did. Her trainers worked well as she chased down a teenage boy who had hidden underneath a car. She caught the mother and daughter, who were carrying things from the car to their home, then the two boys inside, who cut her. That didn't matter in the end, however, as they all died. And soon there was no more food.

So, after months of feeding, they all walked off, following the scent of food. The horde grew, then splintered as some wandered off to follow other meals. As they swallowed up villages, towns and cities, the horde grew. Among them was Zoe. She was now staring in the direction of a meal. No one else stopped because they were facing the wrong way, but she couldn't get in. Zoe couldn't climb, so all she could do was walk and, when the energy was there, she would run.

A big, fat man knocked into her, spinning her around, and she ended back inside the horde. All thought of the meal and house was gone, but now she had two thoughts: one was to feed, the other was that her trainers were dirty.

Chapter 7

'Well, that was bloody weird,' I said to myself as I watched Miss Fitness Zombie get moved along by the horde. It was so strange, as I had felt sure that she was staring right at me. I shivered like a shitting dog. I always loved that saying. It took what felt like hours for the stream of dead to finally pass by. I waited for a bit longer and then finally ran off to the toilet, to rid myself of the things I'd been too uptight to give up during the night.

I cooked up some pasta and ate it with a squeeze of tomato sauce, just to save on the homemade sauce. After finishing the fine food, I realised I needed a friend. Maybe a dog, who would happily clean my dishes for me. Then all I would need do was rinse and repeat. I know, ladies – I'm a catch.

Putting the pistol in my waistband, I crept around the perimeter of the fence. The pasta I had eaten did try and do a curtain call at the sight of all the bodily waste that the horde had dropped on its journey to Lord knew where. I walked around and found it all clear, but I did lock my eyes onto what appeared to be a farmhouse in the distance. I couldn't see the house properly due to the distance and the tears filling my eyes due to the foul smell. I could see metallic barns – from a TV programme I had once seen, I presumed they were used to house cows and other animals.

I mused for a moment about the time of day, but I reckoned I had enough time to walk over and back. Hopefully, the property would be fully stocked, or at the least have some more toilet paper. You never can have enough of that bad boy. I ran back inside to grab a bottle of water and an empty bag, then I started my walk over the now overgrown field, which looked like wheat. Well, it matched the picture on the Weetabix box – although, due to the rainstorms and the fact it had not been harvested, the crops were now lying flat in many places with the smell of rot loitering above. It took a while to get over the two fields separating me from the farmhouse, and then a couple of falls and swearing and physical assaults upon said wheat.

As I got closer to my goal, I used my commando training and crouched over and walked closer to the old stone wall which surrounded the farm. When I say training, I mean Call of Duty of course. There was nothing around that I could see – nothing living or moving, that is. The wind was blowing litter about the yard, but that was it. My nerves were taut as I climbed over the wall, sending small chips of the stone onto the concrete.

I crept over to the closest barn, and for some reason I had the theme tune from *Jaws* in my head. Damn my imagination. The open-air barn housed a tractor and other farm equipment, which looked more like torture equipment to me, but what did I know? I ran to the next metallic barn and found it stinking to high heaven. I poked my head around and was nearly sick; it seemed that a whole load of cows had been set upon. They'd left hardly anything. There were also a few zombie bodies littered about amongst the blood-covered straw and carcasses. The cows must have got some good licks in against their attackers before they were torn to shreds.

I went around to the sealed back of the cow barn and moved closer to the house. It still amazed me that I hadn't seen any walkers about the area. I was now facing the back door of the farmhouse; the curtains were all closed, but the old wooden door was open. Now here's a question: Why did the farmhouse have a normal solid door, while the Colonel's house had a stable door? People were weird.

I crept closer now with the *Mission Impossible* tune in my head and I had now pulled out my soon-to-be-cleaned gun. The safety catch was now off and a bullet was in the chamber. I noticed a bloody handprint on the door. Now my bowels were one scream away from liquefying. The gun was shaking in my hands as I walked into the dark house. I silently screamed 'TORCH!'

My eyes darted about in the gloom.

'What am I doing?' I muttered.

There wasn't a single noise. I drew back the curtains, allowing some light into the kitchen, but not enough. I ventured further in, but what saved my nerves was the large torch I spotted on the table. You gotta love farmers. I tried to adopt the same stance as the police on TV by holding the torch in the same hand as the gun – which is all well and good until you have to open a door.

As it turned out, there was no one home, just bloodied handprints around the house. However, I could now confidently say that this gun worked. And yes, I hit what I fired at. Something had run at me in the lounge. Rest in peace, Mr Tiddles. Oh, and rest in peace to my boxer shorts, trousers and socks. I was still hoping to save the boots.

I did open the fridge, despite my previous rules, and saw three cans of cider. In the bag they went. Then I moved on to the cupboards, which held a good assortment of cans and dried food stuffs, which filled the bag to its brim. By now, the sun was getting low in the sky, sending a red hue over the house. I would come back tomorrow first thing for a better search. Maybe the farmer had a gun, and a car that I could learn to drive in.

I walked back to my house with a full bag of food in one hand and sixteen packs of toilet roll in the other. I was now wearing a dirty pair of overalls, having removed my now soiled garbs. That bloody cat really did scare me.

The walk back was okay. I only fell once when I tried to leap the fence and caught my trailing leg on the uppermost strand of barbed wire. It had been my fault – the light was failing and I was trying to hurry. Maybe it was the ghost of Tiddles, the little shit. I unlocked the back door, stepped in quickly and closed it behind me, locking it securely, thanks to the spare sets of keys I had found in the office drawer.

The bag and toilet rolls were dropped and I headed off to have a bath. I lit the candle in the main bedroom and kicked off the wellies I had taken from the other house, as my others were in soak. I took out the cat culler and threw it onto the bed, watching it bounce as I had done many times before. But something was different; instead of bouncing further onto the bed, the weapon came back towards me, then down onto the floor and the plush carpeting. My eyes followed its movement.

Maybe this is what Jeff Goldblum was explaining to Laura Dern in *Jurassic Park*. Chaos theory. The gun landed in the most unhelpful position – handle down, barrel facing me. BANG! *Who turned out the lights?* was my last thought in the darkness.

This wasn't the first time I awoke in darkness and pain, but reading this you would know that, anyway. My face was killing me, so I stupidly moved my hand to touch it,

'FUCKKK!' I hollered into the darkness, as my hand came away slick. I was either crying like a baby, or I was bleeding. I begged it be the former.

I felt around and found the weapon. I was one second away from casting it into the night, but that was how I had got into this position in the first place. Where was Olga when you needed her? I took hold of the gun and pushed it under the wooden bedframe, then began searching the floor for the rogue candle. Time seemed to stand still as I grappled in the dark until I finally found the candle. I must have fallen on it as I fell – that would explain the pain in my ribs. It truly was a day of days.

The lighter was still on the nightstand, and soon there was light. I didn't want to make more than one trip, so I stripped slowly as my body and face were hurting. I took a breath and walked into the en-suite with the candle and then stood still. I truly was living through a horror film.

I must have moved my head at the last second as the bullet cut a furrow from the edge of my mouth past my eye, costing me a piece of my hair line. The speed and heat of the bullet had cauterised the wound, but infection was a real probability. I placed the candle by the sink and jumped in the bath, washing all the residue from the Tiddles killing. I really hoped that the cats wouldn't start protesting around me, saying 'felines matter'.

Within minutes I was out and began rummaging through the bathroom cabinet, before realising I had emptied it earlier and taken all the contents downstairs, just in case I had to bolt.

'Fuck's sake,' I growled before drying myself off. Wrapping the towel around me, I grabbed the candle and headed down the stairs, losing the towel halfway down. However, I was on a mission and so, with dick swinging freely, I entered the kitchen and moved quickly to light the rest of the candles. I would need to find more, too.

I grabbed a bottle of water, some paracetamol and antibiotics – not sure why the lady of the house had them, maybe she associated with a dirty sort? But I guess we will never know. There was a tube of antiseptic cream. I used just enough to cover the wound so that I still had enough for the morning.

I sat at the kitchen table and felt as low as it was humanly possible. I was stuck in a strange house, all on my own in the middle of the

Zombie Apocalypse. I had almost blown my face off with a World War II pistol, and a German one at that. Maybe that was karma telling me not to open that cabinet upstairs, which still taunted me. *Damn you to hell*, I thought. Sleep claimed me after adding wine into the mix of painkillers, but at least it was a dreamless sleep.

The next morning started with a scream, and yes it was me. Somehow, I had slept, face down, on the kitchen table, which the congealed blood and gunk had adhered to. As a result, when my body began to awaken, it tore itself free. With more emotions than a mother holding her first born after hours of labour, I sobbed like a little bitch, and instantly threw any available tablets down my gullet.

Once my usual ablutions were taken care of, I emptied the dirty bath and offered my thanks to the stars and heavens when it refilled once again with clean, but freezing cold, water. My wound looked something from *Nightmare on Elm Street*. But, with water and cotton swabs thank to Mrs Colonel, I cleaned it, reapplied the cream, then covered it with a layer of gauze to protect it.

After coffee and a cereal bar that I had found yesterday, I did my normal circuit. Everything was secure, though my ribs and face were thrumming with pain. But life must go on – the days were getting colder and shorter, and soon the early morning frost would be coming. Time to start gathering wood, and more food. Thankfully, with the water butt and the typical English winter I should have plenty of water, but I filled up spare water bottles with freshly boiled water just in case. Who knew trying to stay alive would be so problematic?

I dressed in the late Colonel's clothes and boots and, despite my negative feelings, I took the gun and my now empty bag and plodded back over the fields to the farm. This time, I placed my feet like a cat burglar in the Tower of London, and only fell the once on the weather-beaten crops.

The farm still looked quiet as I hopped over the wall to enter the yard, but this time I moved around the outskirts of the farm first. It was overgrown. There was a chicken coop that had been torn apart by the dead. I was chuffed to find an old, beaten-up Land Rover. It was unlocked, but no keys. Hopefully, they were in the house. I carried on my search around the property, but it was devoid of anything worthwhile, so I headed slowly back into the resting place of Tiddles and reclaimed my soaked boots, hoping that the essence of looseness of bowels would have dissipated overnight. I threw them outside to dry, despite the lack of sunlight.

In the kitchen was a bowl of keys, which I presumed must be for the Land Rover and the tractor. There was also a small chubb brass key. Hope returned and the search continued. I managed to gather more clean clothes and undergarments, even though they were too big, but I wouldn't be going anywhere near a town with that horde wandering about.

'Score!' I shouted out as I discovered a slim, metal gun safe in a cupboard in the hallway.

The chubb key went into the lock smoothly and the door swung open.

'RESULT!' There stood a double-barrelled shotgun, the type where the barrels were side by side. Next to that was a small rifle with a scope. On the shelf above were large boxes of shotgun shells, and smaller boxes for bullets that I presumed were for the rifle. Cats beware, I was now a true apocalypse warrior.

I removed the weapons and ammo and placed them all on the kitchen table, along with the clothes. My ribs and face were aching now, so I popped some more tablets and carried on emptying the larder and cupboards of everything. Hopefully, I would have enough for the winter. It was good that the winters were normally snow free, and even when we did have snow it was only for a week or two. Touch wood.

I took the rest of the keys from the bowl and headed outside into the wonderful grey day. I made my way towards the Land Rover. It was a manual, which would be a problem, though I did manage to crash the last one within seconds of driving it, and that was an automatic. But then I blew it up, so what good was it?

The filth-encrusted driver's door creaked open and I was knocked back by the smell of manure. My nasal cavity was assaulted, but it *was* a farm vehicle after all. For one second my eyes strayed to the tractor, but my imagination fed me some 'what if?' scenarios that didn't end well for me, or anything that found itself in my path. One of the keys did fit the ignition of the Land Rover and, holding my breath, I turned it. A light on the dashboard did come on, but I didn't know what it meant.

Remembering TV programmes about cars, I waggled the gearstick to make sure it wasn't in gear, then looked at the faded markings on the top.

'One, two, three, four, reverse,' I muttered and then saw one more peddle, which I presumed was the clutch.

I turned the key again and it made a noise. The engine was turning over but it wasn't catching, so I stopped trying, waited for a moment, and then tried again. It was on the third time of trying that the engine finally caught and it fired into life. I allowed myself a smile for this minor victory.

I pressed the accelerator, making the engine rev nicely. It was ticking over roughly, but at least it didn't stop. The fuel gauge was at half a tank, which reassured me. I remembered my dad always saying that, when he first had a car, on cold mornings he used to leave it running to warm the engine up and charge up the battery. At least he was useful for something.

'Rest in peace, Mum and Dad,' I muttered and stared at all the pedals and the gearstick. I took a deep breath, pressed down the clutch and pushed the gearstick forwards and to the left, into first gear. Then, as gently as I could, I increased the revs and released the clutch at the same time and in the same slow manner.

The stinking vehicle seemed to rise and leant forwards, and I thought Christmas was coming. But then it stalled. I tried to calm my breathing and not shout at the butterfly that had fluttered by and caused it to stall.

The colourful bastard, mocking me with its grace. The Land Rover started again, and I went through the same procedures, and again that dick of an insect had spread his bad karma around me. My face and ribs were banging. I reasoned that it must be the stress, or else that flying dick was spreading a deadly contagion to finally kill me and my kind. Who says an imagination is a wonderful thing?

The whole truck was vibrating nearly as much as my temper. As I took my hands off the steering wheel, my left hand slammed into something that sent pain flying up my arm. I winced and looked down at the thing, and the thing was the handbrake sitting there all happy and proudly fully engaged. I growled like a feral dog.

'SON OF A BITCH!' I then screamed in pain thanks to the bullet-firing piece of shit. I took hold of the handbrake with my left hand and, using my thumb, pressed in the soiled white button on the end. With a slight jostle, the handbrake released and dropped towards the cigarette-end and shit-covered floor.

After all that and a couple of stalls later, I was finally driving around the farm. I even made it into second gear, and while I was moving, too. It was on my fourth journey around the farm that I saw a flash of orange by the house. I slowed/stalled the old Land Rover and pulled on the accursed handbrake. With a groan of pain, I slipped out and opened a metal mesh door, which was covered in ivy, and there sat four glorious and large gas bottles.

'Praise be!'

Clearly there weren't any gas mains around this area, but then that's the country for you. Only two of the containers were full, the others were only half full, but they would be worthwhile taking at some point. But all this would have to wait until I was able to move without screaming in pain like a little girl.

The truck was loaded. It had no rear seats, just a large space in the back littered with plastic sacks and covered with a canvas top, which was torn in many places. The sacks were thrown to the ground and I placed some of the late farmer's overcoats onto the floor of the truck to protect my new acquisitions – the clothes, the guns, ammo and the foodstuffs.

Locking the farm door after me, I drove down the driveway. It was only a quick journey, but what took longer was the fact I had to climb the bloody gate at the Colonel's property and walk all the way up the drive, then into the Colonel's house to get the BLOODY KEY TO OPEN THE MOTHERFUCKING GATE!!!

It was the little things like this that pushed me to breaking point. There is a saying that goes 'roll with the punches', and that I can do. Unless it's a gang of ten thumping you at the same time, in which case you end up boss-eyed and bloodied, and that was the way I was feeling and looking right now. I knew I had to act and think smarter, otherwise this world would consume me.

The drive up to the house went okay, though it was a jerky one. I managed to park/abandon the vehicle at the front of what I was now imagining to be my house. Once the engine was turned off, the world fell silent once again, except for the noise of my feet crunching on the gravel-laden driveway as I made my way back down to chain up the front gate. Yes, it was an extra journey, but once I got the thing going I didn't want to stop it until I had to.

'Feel the burn,' I muttered to myself as my ribs reminded me of the damage I had caused to myself.

Slowly but surely, I brought everything into 'my' house. I listed all the items and put them away. Being paranoid, I decided to hide all the guns. Call it walking dead phobia, but there would always be some who will want to take anything that you have gathered. It was now a dog-eat-dog world, and I would not be seen to be weak.

'Oh, cool. Pringles!'

As the sun went down on another productive day, I ate some crisps with a glass of merlot. Just call me Bond, James Bond. The days were getting shorter and there was a chill in the morning air. I figured it must be October time, so I made a list of jobs to do in the next few days – although I needed to rest my face and ribs, too, which was tricky. I laughed a lonely chuckle as the cocktail of painkillers I had taken took hold, and I enjoyed the last rays of sunlight bathing my lounge in orange light.

Chapter 8

Sometime later (possibly a month)

'SNOW! WHAT THE HELL!' I screamed out of my bedroom window.

For as far as I could see, the whole countryside was blanketed by God knows how many feet of the bloody stuff. With a shake of my head, I wandered off to have a ball-shrinking wash. By now, all this time spent on my own had made me into a new man. I even had a motherfucking six pack. I was RIPPED! Shame there were no women.

I slipped into my recently cleaned boxers and a pair of overalls and went to the spare room. As had now become routine, I picked up a lump hammer and slammed it into the chisel, which had pride of place sticking out from the door seam on the gun cabinet.

'One day, my beauty, you will open up like a flower to spread your seed unto the world,' I said and shuddered at my words. I had spent too much time alone. I gave the cabinet another hit for luck, driving the iron weapon in just a little further.

For weeks now, I had been trying to penetrate the cabinet, driving anything I could find in deep. *Jesus, where is my mind at? Everything seems to have sexual undertones. I need porn.* Who'd have thought an army bloke's house would be devoid of spanking material? What was the world coming to? Oh yes, a zombie apocalyptic waste ground.

Though he seemed to be a very pious gentleman and the only vice he held onto was the fermented grape, the Colonel did have a lot of helpful books about hunting, trapping and survival. What saved my life were the books and army manuals about shooting and gun care. So, with his help, I discovered that the rifle I had found at the farm was a .22 rimfire rifle with a scope, with two hundred rounds – of which I had used thirty-odd while learning how to use it.

The weapon enabled me to hunt for pheasants, rabbits – and that shit of a squirrel. Well, it looked like him. The latter tasted like shit, but at least the rifle was quieter than the shotgun, which was soooo loud. It also destroyed the rabbit (maybe I had been a bit too close?). I decided I would save it for when the putrid dead ones turned up again.

Since the first day when that major horde had appeared, and when that scary and strangely hot yoga pant-wearing zombie stared at me, they had since moved past twice. But, as before, they moved along slowly like a river and, thanks to the gate, they just carried on by. My brain told me there must be several barricades somewhere for the horde to be sent back my way, unless they were several different ones. That thought alone used up a fair bit of my dwindling toilet paper supply.

As the days passed, I had tightened up my chores, so that every night I brought in enough water just in case it froze. Apart from that, I was stuck indoors for a while. There were a few pheasants hanging up in the garden shed, but the crisp chill in the air would keep them fresh for a few more days yet.

I saw no point in doing anything today, apart from airing the place out, as it did have a certain funk to it. The 'funk' had, of course, already been there when I arrived, as no smell ever came from me… promise. So today would be eating cold pigeon with pasta and red wine.

'I miss Red Bull,' I muttered as I stripped down the rifle. That comment made my heart jump in panic (hold a grudge much), as the memory of the *riding the bull* episode came flooding back to me. With a smile on my lips I thumped my chest to encourage my worried heart 'keep going baby!'

My bath water was only a couple of days old, so I put a few buckets of fresh, soft snow into it, just to freshen it up a bit. Thankfully, wherever the water was coming from was still working and clean, and if it stopped I would be in trouble. If it stopped raining, I would have to leave, though if it stopped raining completely I knew I wouldn't be in England.

The gas was lasting well as I had managed to grab the cylinders from the farm. I will admit, it took a while, but I will describe it in the form of bullet points only. No spanner. Found spanner. Dropped cylinder on foot. Kicked said cylinder, hurt foot. Tied cylinders into Land Rover. Made it home. Untied cylinders. Watched cylinder roll off truck and down the driveway. Cried.

Slowly, my food supply began to dwindle and I was starting to worry. The next morning gave me something else to worry about. After washing myself, I wandered around my bedroom gazing out of the large window. It was when I was showing my family jewels to the winter wonderland outside that I saw movement down the bottom of the driveway by the gate.

I ducked down and watched through some binoculars that the Colonel had squirrelled away. A man in a camouflage jacket was climbing over the gate. Was this a rescue? Then I watched him slip off the wood and fall, face first, into a small and well-placed snow drift. I quickly threw on my overalls, yelping as the zip caught my curliest of curly hairs.

'Mama…' I sobbed and took the overalls off. I then put on some safe boxers, then socks, and then the overalls again. Then I was hopping towards the stairs, trying to put boots on as I did so.

I had left the face destroyer of a pistol in the bedside cabinet. Better safe than sorry – I already looked like a criminal. The stairs creaked as I made my way down and picked up the .22 rifle from the kitchen counter.

I opened the French doors at the back and snuck out. I could still hear the man walking/slipping up the driveway. Well, I could hear his expletives, anyway. Knowing where he was, I hurried past the kitchen door and to the corner of the house. Then I edged past the Land Rover, trying not to think about the puddle of black stuff that had formed underneath it. Not a good sign, methinks.

Like any good action film, I moved the bolt action on the gun, which wasted a bullet as it flew into the air and was lost forever in the snow. The man stood stock still upon hearing the noise and moved his head around quickly.

'Morning,' I said coldly, which was correct as I hadn't put a coat or gloves on, and the bloody gun was cold.

The man was about 5'3, balding, maybe in his forties, shaped like an egg. I noticed the devil's own red hair poking out from his woolly cap.

'Oh shit...' he said when he saw me. 'Hello, mate. Err... don't shoot!' He tried to speak in a manly way, but failed. But then, would I be any different? Of course I would.

'I won't, unless I have to,' I replied in my best Clint Eastwood spaghetti Western drawl.

He frowned. 'You what? I didn't understand what you said.'

I sighed. *I hate people, I really do.* 'I won't shoot unless I have to, all right!!'

'Yeah, cool, mate,' he replied. 'I'm just cold and hungry. Trying to find a place to chill until the snow pisses off.' He tried to smile, but it wasn't a nice sight. His mouth looked like a neglected graveyard, with a multitude of colours. It made me shudder.

I dropped the barrel of my gun a little to show I wasn't a mass murderer. 'What's your name, mate? And where did you come from?'

'David Summers,' he said, 'but you can call me Zombie Killer.' I rolled my eyes. 'I lived in Stokenchurch, a few miles away,' he continued. 'We were driven out. I was trying to make it to Aylesbury for safety.'

Never heard that one before. Most people had fled that town for safety. 'Okay, we can talk more inside. But no funny business,' I said and walked sideways, back to the French doors. 'Wipe your feet, and I'll get a fire going.'

The man came in and did as I ordered. I set about working on the open fire in the lounge. I didn't normally do this, as the smoke would give away my position to anyone in the vicinity. Call me Mr Paranoid, but I didn't want him to know quite yet that I had gas. About ten minutes later, the fire was crackling away happily.

'You want a coffee, Dave?'

'David,' he replied. 'And yes please, milk and two sugars.' He was sitting on the flower-adorned sofa and smiled at me with a 'special needs' kind of look.

'Err, did you bring a cow with ya?' I said.

He frowned. 'No. Why?'

My knuckles itched. I should've shot him. 'It's the Zombie Apocalypse. There's no milk, man. I have tea or coffee for now, but no sugar,' I lied.

He flushed red. 'Oh, yeah, sorry,' he said and shuffled his still dirty boots on my carpet. 'Err, we were living on a farm which had cows.

Sorry...' By now I had wandered away. He had said 'we' again. I'll have to ask Killer about that.

I boiled up some water and made myself a tea with sugar (fuck you) and the Zombie Killer a coffee and headed back into the lounge, only to be assaulted by a godawful smell. David not Dave was sitting there with his walking boots and socks off and wiggling his bare toes at the fire.

'Fuck me, you stink,' I said.

He shuffled on the couch. 'Sorry, but my feet were frozen and soaked through,' he mumbled with his head down, like I was his mum chiding him. I inwardly tutted and handed him the coffee. I then sat down on the smaller sofa, trying to ignore the smell while enjoying my sweetened tea.

'So... David, tell me about yourself,' I said and watched his eyes dart about. Guilt or a medical condition? How would I know?

He warmed his hands on the steaming hot beverage. 'Well, you know my name. I'm forty-three and a Sagittarius. I was in Number Three Parachute Regiment for ten years, then I jumped from job to job til this shit happened. We managed to clear out any deadheads who came near the farm, but that didn't last, so that's how I ended up here.' He took a long sip of his drink and grimaced at the harsh-tasting liquid.

I nodded as he talked. Some of the things he said just didn't add up. I couldn't imagine an ex-Para not being able to climb a gate. 'So, what happened to your friends, then?' I said.

'They were killed,' David said with tears filling his eyes. 'It was horrible.'

I took another sip from my tea. 'Sorry, mate,' I replied. 'Bloody zombies.' I noticed that he didn't verbally reply, but just nodded. So I told him my story, minus certain aspects, like Red Bull, and a certain fetching red dress. Oh, and crashing cars.

'So, you just got the rifle, then?' he said, eyeing the gun as it leant up against the ornate stone fireplace.

'No, I have a shotgun, too, but it makes too much noise,' I said, deciding to throw him a bone. 'There's a gun safe upstairs, but there wasn't a key for it. It's been the bane of my existence.'

He smiled at that, and then tapped his cheek. 'What happened there?' he said, pointing at my face.

I could have said that a pistol had dropped on the floor and a ghost of a dead German army officer had tried to brain me. 'I was going house to house getting food. Someone took a pot shot at me.' I lied, but he seemed to believe it.

The conversation stilled, but then he looked up. 'Can I stay here, mate? I'll help out, hunt or gather wood.' He almost begged and I could see the desperation painted across his face.

'Sure,' I replied, 'we need to find a new place to scavenge. With two of us, our supplies won't last long.' Inwardly, I was proud at how I sounded. Call me Bear Grylls, bitch.

For the next couple of days, David shadowed me on my normal routines. He spent a whole hour shouting and screaming at the gun safe before crying himself to sleep in the same room. I was glad it wasn't just me who was bat shit crazy.

The snow was rained away, which allowed us to fill up all the toilet cisterns. Thankfully, the drains were still working. This world would be even harder if I had to defecate in a bucket. David not Dave worked well, but I wasn't too confident when he offered to clean the guns – just like the good old days in Iraq.

He got irate enough when he couldn't get the rifle back together again, though. 'We never had rifles like this piece of shit in the service,' he said and stomped off to cut more firewood.

That evening, we shared a candlelit meal together that consisted of tuna and pasta in a red wine and tomato sauce. The lady's homemade sauce was coming to an end, amongst other things. No, it wasn't romantic, so get your head out of the gutter.

'Tony,' he said, 'on my way here, I saw another farm. It was set back further into the wood, but the sign did say farm on it.' David pointed in the direction he had come from – or over the hill. Who knew? We were sitting in the bloody dark.

I frowned at him. It was an expression I seemed to be using way too often with this older bloke. 'How come you came here and not there, if you passed it on the way?' I probed and saw him flush.

'I heard noises coming from it and it was dark,' he admitted, and I saw his hands were shaking. 'This place seemed friendlier, almost.' He forced a smile.

'Okay, we'll walk there in the morning,' I said as I planned out the day. 'You can take the shotgun, and I the rifle.'

He nodded in agreement. 'What about the Land Rover?' he said 'Why don't we take that?'

'Nope, it will bring every deadhead for miles this way,' I replied. 'We'll only use it if we have to, okay?' I took a sip of wine, which was starting to get on my tits. We needed to find something else to drink. 'That's why I always keep the gate locked. When the horde comes past, they just stagger on by. So never open the gate unless it's necessary, okay?'

That night, I fell asleep to the screams and rants as David tried to get into the gun cabinet. Somehow, I found it soothing. The next morning, we donned our rucksacks and weapons and headed out. I left the pistol at home. I didn't need another accident, especially as I watched my companion stretching with the loaded shotgun leaning against his crutch, the barrels aiming at his babymakers. But he was company.

We headed out together, side by side, down the driveway. As I held his gun, David climbed over the gate like a paraplegic, though they had more pride than this man. I supressed my girlish giggle as he slipped again, separating his babymakers either side of the wooden gate. I waited for his tears and swearing to die down and we hit the road. It was a clear, chilly day and, though I loathe to say it, it was dead quiet. With no cars or planes now, it was as quiet as a graveyard. I'm so shit at analogies.

The tarmac was littered with rotten foliage with accompanying branches blown off the overhanging trees, which seemed to be going rogue. Maybe it was time for nature to reclaim the land as its own? We were going to be so buggered if things turned out to be more like Fangorn Forest in the *Lord of the Rings*. I missed TV.

As we walked, my thoughts stayed with TV and a sexually explicit butt-spanking romp with an ethereal Elven maiden. However, David not Dave talked about his time fighting the Taliban in the desert of Iraq. It did sound plausible, though it took him two minutes to break the shotgun open. We are so dead. He did try and wear the cartridge belt across his chest as per a Mexican bandit.

It felt like several hours by the time we made it to the turning he had told me about. The sign, that had once been white, was now tinged green thanks to the lack of care by the probably dead owner.

'Cock Farm,' I read and looked at Rambo, who was scratching his nuts with a stick. 'You serious about this, mate? It's either a brothel or a chicken farm.'

I waited on the king of wit to answer me, but all I received back was a grunt. I looked down the lane. It was overgrown, so not even a spot of light pierced through the canopy above. All it needed was a wind blowing the leaves and a wolf howling off in the distance. With an audible click, the safety catch on my rifle was flicked off and I headed off into the darkness and our possible doom.

'Come on, David,' I said. 'They say death always likes company.' I laughed by myself, once again.

We headed into the darkness and every horror film played itself out in my mind. Every leaf that cracked underfoot sounded loud enough to raise the dead. I cursed myself that I hadn't brought one of my few working torches. Then again, we were here now. Five minutes later, I saw the farm cottage bathed in the winter sun. I signalled David not Dave to stand still so we could listen for any sounds.

It was quiet. 'Shall we go back?' David said with a shaky voice, making me shoot him a glare. I shook my head.

'No,' I said. 'You go to the left and check all the windows, and I'll head right.' I waved my hand towards the direction I wanted him to go. I did feel like I had fallen out of Call of Duty, which did make me chuckle and brought a confused look from my apocalypse partner in crime.

As I crept around the overgrown farm courtyard, I knew our goal was the house. I noticed a large shed, which looked too bloody long. With the hot summer and now the cold weather, most of the smells of rotting animals had dissipated somewhat. The windows of the house were filthy with God knows what. No surprise there, but it meant we couldn't see inside. David lifted the gun as he saw me and, for the briefest of moments, I thought the dick would pull the trigger. I survived this time. I guess it was his army training kicking in (my arse!).

'What now?' he asked as his eyes shot around in all directions. I didn't need this shit. He was losing his nerve.

I walked up to the nearest window and stuck the stock of my gun through it, showering myself in shards of glass. For once, I wasn't hurt. David was just about to berate me, but I signalled him to shut the fuck up. I leant in, trying to listen for any signs of movement, but all I could hear was my heavy breathing after having walked on the flat for a minute or two. I know I was unfit, but c'mon.

'Sounds clear, Dave,' I said with a smile. 'Check the doors and kick them in.'

'David.'

I rolled my eyes and wandered off to the front door. How did a dickhead like that even know how to spell army, let alone serve in it?

The front door was locked, so I aligned my boot up with the lock. I did a couple of practice swings and then, on the third swing, I slammed my foot against the door as hard as I could, putting all my weight behind it. There was no splintering of wood. No sense of victory. Just the blinding pain as I hit the deck.

'Fuckkkkkk! My sodding knee,' I muttered and rolled away.

'You okay, mate?' David asked as he swung the now unlocked door outwards. He saw me holding my knee and then laughed. 'You tried to kick it inwards! No, that's funny.' He then walked into the house, leaving the door sticking outwards mockingly.

I managed to get back up and it hurt like a bitch, but soon loosened up. He did come back out to help me up, and we both stepped inside the house.

'Anyone about?' I called out to David as I started to open the cupboards. Once again, it was your typical rural kitchen. I saw a gas bottle outside by the big shed.

David didn't answer, so I turned to him and he nodded.

'Yeah, an old couple upstairs with a shit load of empty pill bottles and a note,' he said sadly and wiped tears from his eyes. Then he began to help me go through the cupboards. There was basically nothing left. The occupants were old and had been nearly out of food.

He walked and I limped out of the house with just three cans of food and some gravy granules. There was a shotgun and a few cartridges. The gun was rusted to buggery, but Gi Joe claimed he could get it working. I reckoned his time on this earth was coming to an end.

We wandered to the shed and that's where we, as a team, voided our stomachs. The corpses of hundreds of chickens and turkeys were strewn on the ground. It truly was a sad sight knowing that they had a long lingering death.

Chapter 9

Date and time: just don't ask

Well, fuck me. David not Dave did it. He fired the shotgun from Cock Farm. Still love that name – which did, in fact, turn out to be the family name. Rest in peace Cocks (chuckle). We managed to retrieve five half-filled 47 kg gas bottles from around the farm, which we took back with the help of the now struggling Land Rover.

The winter cold snap had gone away and now it was just chilly and wet. God bless England. It was still cool enough to hang game out in the shed, though. As the days clicked by, our eternal struggle with the resident cabinet continued with no joy. There had better be a cannon in there, especially with all the blood and tears we had lost. That night, we discovered that neither of us liked hare. The taste was okay, but the after effects put a real dent in our toilet paper supply, not to mention the couple of hours spent ripping out and burning the fecal-splattered carpet and David's trousers. That was a bad night.

The supposed ex-army man was beginning to grow on me. You just had to filter out the bullshit. We had a night on the booze as I had found a bottle of whisky in the barn of the first farm I had gotten to. The owner must have been a closet alcoholic to have had it hidden so well. So David and I drank it dry, and that's when I learnt the truth about his last abode. It wasn't a zombie that had caused the problem. It turned out to be a gang of some sort who had slaughtered his whole group, so he ran.

I felt for him, but I'm sure a fate worse than death would have been in store for any woman caught by such a group of thugs. After that admission, I decided not to ask any further questions about his army career.

The next morning began slowly. We washed out the guttering on the shed and emptied the water to stop it going all funky, in preparation for fresh rain to refill it. We had enough water already boiled and bottled to keep us going for weeks, and the water in the taps was still running – though the colour was a bit questionable, so that definitely was just for washing. And, for a treat, I allowed us to use the gas for a nice hot bath.

After the night of 'The mass toilet paper migration', we decided to raid more nearby properties. However, the best thing about the countryside was also the worst thing – it was desolate. Not like in America or Australia, but close enough. Using the Land Rover wasn't a good idea as it sounded like hell, especially as my housemate took it upon himself to fix it. Now, I'm not mechanically minded, but even I know you shouldn't have bits left over when you put an engine back together again. I did have to swallow my anger as he chucked those bits away, claiming the engine didn't need them 'as they had over engineered it'.

So, we walked for miles and, though my fitness had improved and my knee had healed, my colleague, old *one lung David*, complained all the way. I told him that it needed to be done and that, since our truck was no longer trustworthy, it was foot power until we found a replacement.

However, we discovered that most car batteries these days were dead and, with no way of recharging said batteries, we were stuck to walking.

We arrived at several smallholdings, which the horde had been through. Everything was dead or had been destroyed by their vast numbers, but house by house we collected bits and bobs that we needed to aid our survival – mainly toilet paper, soap, tinned food, pasta and rice. We found several shotguns and also cartridges, which brought our stock of bullets to three hundred for our arsenal of weapons.

There were gas bottles, too, but just no way of getting them home. However, the main score for me was sourced in the garage of a dilapidated house, which brought some hope into my life: a Law of Rhythm pamphlet. Yes, we are talking porn in the form of an old school magazine. After all this death and destruction, there, like a beacon in the night, sat an unsoiled magazine.

'Sorry, David, this baby is mine,' I muttered and stuffed it into my back pack. That day, I nearly ran home, and I had a very nice, long sleep that night with hope in my heart for once.

> *It was the best of times, it was the worst of times, it was the age of wisdom, it was the age of foolishness, it was the epoch of belief, it was the epoch of incredulity, it was the season of light, it was the season of darkness, it was the spring of hope, it was the winter of despair, we had everything before us, we had nothing before us.*

That quote from *A Tale of Two Cities* summed life up quite nicely. David, despite my initial misgiving, was doing quite well hunting for food in the woods and keeping the guns cleaned and oiled. But that was when I made my fateful error.

I gave David my Luger to clean as I had kept it locked away since his arrival. He was over the moon, just as I had been until it had tried to kill me. Within a moment of me passing it over and asking him to clean and check the thing, it was in pieces and scattered across the kitchen table. I left him to it as I took another gun out into the woods to see what I could get. The weather was on the turn, so I had guessed it was at least March. It was slightly warmer and raining a lot more, but in England that could even be summer.

It had been a good day so far. I had bagged myself a cock pheasant and it felt nicely heavy in my hand. As I entered the kitchen, David was still beavering away at the German pistol. I stood at the sink and cut the breast from the bird to fry up later. It took too long to pluck the thing, and there wasn't much meat on the bird apart from the breast meat, anyhow.

I watched on as David happily put the gun back together again.

'You having fun there, buddy?' I asked.

'This is awesome. How come I haven't seen it before?' David asked, looking up at me.

I tapped my scar. 'It went off and nearly took my face off,' I admitted and sat down opposite him, handing him a coffee that I had brewed. 'Yeah, I know I lied. But it's not something you brag about, is it?'

David chuckled. 'I guess not. Anyway, it should be fine now. I've cleaned every bit and oiled it.' He slammed in the bullet magazine before pulling back the charging slide, which put a bullet in the waiting chamber. 'You have to respect your weapons, Tony,' he added seriously. Then I watched as he clicked on the safety catch. 'There you go, mate. You're ready to go to war.' With that, he slammed the gun down onto the cleaning rags he had used.

I winced as it hit the table. My body jumped as the bullet inside the chamber was hit by the firing pin. I closed my eyes as I was coated in fluids that should never see the light of day, unless you were having an operation where they had the machine that went BING!

My ears were ringing like Quasimodo after he banged Esmeralda in the church tower. I didn't want to open my eyes and witness the scene that I knew awaited me. The bloody pistol truly had the ghost of a German officer still in it. With my eyes shot, I felt my way to the sink and washed my face and stared down into the basin that was now filled with bloodied water accompanied by something that appeared a bit too brain-like for my liking. Immediately, as a rufty-tufty man of the apocalypse, I voided my stomach into the sink.

Taking a deep breath, I turned to see the man I had come to consider as my friend. He was leaning back in the chair with his arms hanging loose by his sides. A ghost of the laugh was still on his lips, but his eyes showed the damage the old bullet had done to his brain as they were both at crazy angles. His head was hanging back, a small hole under his chin and a Jackson Pollock painting up the wall behind him. Somehow, I didn't think there was much call for a picture called 'Midday Brain Splatter'.

It was a dark mood day as I buried David in the garden at sunset. No words were spoken, or tears shed. It was just another death caused by this accursed thing, which had become our life now – or, I should say, *my* life, as once again I found myself alone.

That evening, I polished off the last bottle of the wine from the Colonel's cellar. I truly hoped the man was dead, because he was going to be pissed, especially as I was reduced to wearing his wife's pants. It was a hard life. The next day, my eyes would not leave the stain on the wall where my friend's brains once hung. One foolish act had cost the man his life.

'FUCK YOU!' I screamed as I took all my hurt, sadness and loneliness out on this symbol of everything that was wrong with this new world.

The sledgehammer I wielded that day smashed everything it connected with, all apart from the damned gun cabinet. However, as God was my witness, I would open it and open it I did. As the door finally swung open, albeit wonkily, I dropped to the floor with a thump, covered in tears, sweat, and even a fair amount of snot. It was not a pretty sight.

My eyes searched the cabinet and my heart shattered just like the cabinet itself. There sat an old, beaten-up single barrel shotgun. It looked like the rust alone was the only thing keeping it in one piece. I had spent months daydreaming of all sorts of weaponry sitting in there, waiting for me. *The Walking Dead* this is not. But at least there was a box of fifty more cartridges, which would help in the long run.

As I lay in bed that night, my thoughts were about a roaming gang that went from house to house, killing all in their path – man, woman or child. Oh, and cats. During my time, I have accidently killed a few cats, and before you go shouting that I am starting the Extermination of the Feline Race, I am not. I just have a twitchy trigger and those little fucks tend to jump out at you, and that never ends well for Tiddles or his brethren.

After my normal routine, which now took longer as I was a group of one, I gathered all the weapons and ammo in the kitchen. This consisted of one .22 rifle with just over a hundred bullets, or rounds if I want to sound badass, five shotguns and over three hundred cartridges. Clearly, there were no restrictions on buying those bad boys, which meant I was sitting okay as I was quite handy with the rifle, and getting better with the shotguns. Well, just ask Tiddles – in cat heaven, mind you, as he was no longer here.

I gathered fifty cartridges and a shotgun, along with my rucksack, then traipsed through the muddy fields to the next farm. There, I stored a shotgun, still in its case, and some cartridges and a litre of water. I found a good hiding place in one of the workshops, which I was confident that no one would be able to see. Over the next few days, I did the same at all the surrounding properties we had been to. Call me Mr Paranoid, but if you consider all those zombie films and books, you also have the humans that want to cause you harm. So why not get ready? Especially after what David not Dave had told me about that group of thugs. May he bullshit in peace. I now had weapons, ammo, clothes, food and water in all my safe houses, and all well concealed.

The days started to lengthen, though the rain still came down. It was beginning to warm up as well, so I had a purge on washing my clothes, albeit in cold water. And, as shameful as it was, David's were thrown into the mix. I knew, in the long run, I couldn't stay here for too much longer; it wasn't the home it once was.

It was a week later that the horde came back and with increased numbers. It was the noise and the smell that arrived first. They no longer looked human – their skin was falling off their withering frames, and most of their clothes were gone, which obviously did make me look closer. Yes, I was disgusted by my actions, but boobs are boobs. Get off my back.

Three days after that, there was another surprise. I was in the back garden, having a wash from a soapy bucket, when I heard a crack. I span around and saw a woman standing there with a huge rucksack on her back. She was about five feet ten, slender, with black hair in dreadlocks. She had a nose piercing and a couple of missing teeth which showed when she smiled at me. The woman looked like a traveller, just without a picket sign or a bus to live in.

'Errm, 'ello,' she muttered, eyeing me up and down.

Thankfully, the Colonel's pants were quite a good fit as I stood their wearing just them and holding a soapy sponge. She looked beautiful, if you were willing to overlook the missing teeth and dirty hair.

'Hello, I'm Tony,' I said and freed up a hand, which had been cupping my amorous groin. 'You okay?'

She gave me a look that stopped all amorous thoughts. 'Yeah, I'm shitting rainbows, thanks. Got any food?'

Even her fur-coated, stud-adorned tongue looked kissable. 'Yeah, sure. Follow me,' I said, wandering off with the sponge still dripping bubbles as I walked into the kitchen.

'Fuck…!' I said as I slipped on the floor.

'You okay? You should really get dressed,' she said, dumping her bundle onto the floor, showing off her back that was drenched in sweat. She was a goddess to me.

I pointed to the frying pan, where I had cooked up some pheasant breast that morning so I could snack on it during the day. I was surprised when she delved into it without the words 'No thanks, I'm a vegan' or some troublesome dietary restriction being spouted. It was then I realised I was still wearing nothing but my borrowed pants, so I waved and ran out of the kitchen, drying myself off quickly and dressing even quicker.

'Did you want a coffee?' I almost shouted, making the daughter of Eve jump out of her skin.

'Yeah, sure. Haven't had that in ages,' she said with her full mouth. 'Name is Daphne,' she added and gave a belch, which smelt like angels' kisses. 'You alone in this pad, then?'

Without thinking, I nodded. 'Oh yes, no girlfriend or nothing. Just little old me.' Even though my mind was giving me a mental chiding, every semblance of self-protection had long gone. All she did was smile at me. 'Where are you from?'

'London, originally,' she replied, 'but the city went to shit so quickly me and some friend bailed out.' The possible Princess wiped her mouth on her jacket. 'But they didn't last long, so now it's just me.' She looked around the kitchen. 'What's that stain on ya wall?' she asked and pointed to the Jackson Pollock tribute that adorned the wall and which I had named The Idiot's Brain.

'Damp,' I lied badly. 'You seen anyone else about?'

She shook her dreadlock-covered head, which made her look even more attractive in my mind.

'Nah, fuckin' nothing,' she replied. 'Can I use your bucket? I stink like a badger's arse.' She beamed her gappy smile again.

I nodded and pointed out to the garden. She just rolled her eyes. 'Sorry, yeah, it's all yours,' I muttered.

Daphne pointed a dirt-encrusted finger at me. 'Oi, no staring at my bits. You got me?' She then broke into a cackle of a laugh, which turned into the braying of a donkey as I nodded and blushed even more.

However, as she left I was true to my word and didn't look at her at all... for the first two minutes. I hated myself as she stripped off. She had a massive peace sign tattooed on her back, her underwear was grey... They were cast off quickly, and that was when I started to feel faint. I sat down and tried to equalise my blood storage, and waited for the saucepan to boil the hot water.

After ten minutes, she came back in new clothes and looked clean, apart from her hair – which, in my eyes, looked radiant. Daphne took the coffee I offered her and took a sip.

'Nice?' I asked.

'Bloody nice. Thanks, Tony,' she said with her green eyes filling up. 'It's been so long since I been with someone. Can I kip here, just for a bit?'

Consider my heartstrings pulled. 'Sure, there's a spare room at the front of the house,' I said. 'Unless you wish to kip on the sofa?'

'Fuck, no. Bed would be great,' she said. 'But...' In a flash she had pulled out a knife and was holding it at my throat. Mr Happy had died instantly. 'You come in da room thinkin' ya can fook me, you better think again. Got it?'

I was going to nod, as I was worried about my words upsetting this deadly beauty. However, that was overridden by the thought of the blade slitting my throat.

'You're safe here. Sleep well,' I uttered carefully.

The knife was gone just as fast, but during that second the whole countryside silenced and seemed to wait for another victim to be claimed. When that didn't happen, the sun got bored and started to disappear for the night.

'That's good, then,' replied Daphne. 'I'm fucking knackered. See ya in the morning, mate.' And, with a slap on the back, she was gone, lugging her rucksack upstairs.

I sat there, stunned. The house didn't feel so empty anymore, but something in my head had raised a warning flag. As I lay in my bed and listened to the woman, who I guessed to be in her twenties and snored like an elephant, I did think about what could happen. I knew she had seen the rifle as her eyes had grown wide at the sight. Getting out of bed, I slipped on my gear and headed out, taking the rifle and all the bullets to the farm next door. I locked everything in the gun safe and hid the key with the shotgun and other goodies.

Once back at the house, I settled down to sleep. I felt stupid, but what harm could it do? I didn't know her, or her pert breasts... I shook my head as my thoughts were mixed and it was getting harder to concentrate, but sleep did claim me. But not for long, for I awoke as I felt a warm body next to me.

'What the...?'

'I was cold,' she snapped. 'I just wanna feel warmth for once, okay?' I understood and we both slipped into slumber.

Now, I'm not going into anything else, but our genitals became close friends that night, and in the morning they had a wash together in a cold shower. They then became the best of friends through our second night. It clearly was something that needed to be sorted out, so that now we could concentrate on a friendship or more.

I woke with a strange and cold pressure between my eyes.

'Tony, this has been fun, but now to work,' Daphne said. Panic rose as I realised she had the Luger pressed to my forehead as she straddled my stomach.

'What the fuck? Why are you doing this?' I demanded. Well, okay, begged, as a little bit of wee leaked out of me.

She smiled her toothless smile, which didn't seem so endearing now. 'Survival of the fittest,' she replied. 'Our group saw a fire here a few days back, so I was sent here to check it out.' She gave me a big shit-eating grin. 'I might have gone a bit rogue, but shagging someone new makes a change, don't it?' She leapt off me, making things bounce.

I will admit to the fact that my little head had done the thinking the last couple of days, but I may have gone off her now.

'What now?' I said angrily. 'Take all my stuff and fuck off? Or just kill me?'

'Oh, c'mon lover. Don't be like that,' Daphne said as she dressed herself, then threw my clothes at me. 'Get dressed. The boys will be here soon.' She stood and watched me as I dressed. 'Oh, and Tony…'

She chewed her bottom lip as she looked at me. 'Big Bill might let you live, if you keep our bouncy bouncy fun times a secret. He gets a bit touchy about stuff like that.' She winced at what I imagined was a bad memory coming to the forefront of her mind.

The noise of an engine filtered into the house as we went down the stairs. That didn't bode well for me, along with the temperamental gun being held to my back as the double-crossing bitch happily bounced down the stairs behind me. I stopped before heading out and felt the barrel of the gun pressed into my once fleshy back.

'C'mon baby, let's do this friendly,' she said quietly. 'And if so, you may get to ride the Daphne train again.'

The weather that morning was okay. A faint mist of rain wrapped around us with light grey clouds covering the world. I saw a Land Rover and a transit van come driving towards the house and they popped and banged like they were on their last legs – just like my old truck, which now appeared to have rid itself of its oil. A man, who looked to be at least six feet five, stepped out of the Land Rover, the springs creaking with relief as he exited.

Daphne ran to him excitedly. She attempted to leap into his arms, but a slap from a meaty palm knocked her to the ground. With blood pouring from her nose, she began to cry.

'What did I do wrong, baby?' she screamed, making me wince. 'I did what you said.'

The big man stepped over her and yanked the pistol from her frail hand. He turned it side to side, inspecting it, then smiled at the weapon.

'Fuck me, a Luger,' he said. He then looked at me, then Daphne. 'Yes, you did, petal. But did I tell you to spend two nights fucking him?' He suddenly kicked her in the stomach, causing what contents were in her stomach to be released into the fresh air. This caused other members of his gang to step out of the Land Rover, though the majority poured from the rear of the transit. They began to advance on me and Daphne. They were armed with shotguns and what looked like axe handles. I saw ten minions in total surrounding us, including the man mountain. A fifty-fifty split between men and women, but none pleasing to the eye.

'But I didn't!' Daphne screamed and pointed at me. 'He raped me. Forced me at gunpoint!' I felt the fingers of doom groping at my heart as mist continued to descend, surrounding us like a veil of death. If the Egyptians were right about cats being the guardians of the underworld, I was so boned.

'Daphne, I know rape,' Big Bill smiled and winked at her. 'Screaming "Oh god, oh god" doesn't sound like rape, does it?' He then kicked her again. 'I warned you, bitch. But, no…' With that, he raised the pistol and the Daphne train was dispatched. Her body jumped as the bullets past through her outstretched hand and into her head.

Big Bill walked towards me with a cold smile gracing his face. I saw him tuck the Luger into the waistband of his jeans and I became instantly worried about my boots being covered in essence of bollock. Nothing happened. We locked eyes.

'We need to talk, little man,' Bill stated in a gravelly voice. And, once again, my lights were turned out.

Chapter 10

Date and time are no longer of importance; I had gotten laid

Why could I taste metal? Had one of the Luger's bullets finally found its goal, albeit slower? Then I realised everything was dark and, using all my brain power, I found that my eyes were closed. With a slight crack, my right eyelid opened, followed by its twin brother. I then found myself face to face with an ugly, scarred, blood-covered man – and, if I do say so myself, a very shifty-looking cad if I ever did see one.

Oh, and I seemed to be in the rear bedroom tied to a polished wooden dining chair, sitting opposite the damaged dressing table mirror.

'Well, that's disappointing,' I muttered and looked around. Thankfully, I was not dressed up for some sex-starved psychotic killer. I did not wish to end up as his property – or currency, at that. The plastic zip ties dug into my wrists. I was happy to see they had left my boots on and just tied my legs to the chair with some tights. James Bond I was not, especially as they had already killed the boss's main squeeze.

The mirror told me exactly what I had feared. My nose was busted all to hell and my face had been put through the ringer since coming to this place. The door opened and in strode a woman who had seen too many sunrises and not enough dentists.

'Well, well, look who's awake?' she said, and not with a pleasant voice. It did make me wonder if I had mistakenly guessed her gender, but the massive chest she was sporting told a different story.

It hurt as I smiled at her. 'Hello, my name is Tony. And who are you, my lady?' I asked in my best gigolo impression.

She looked me up and down and laughed. 'Not a chance, twiglet,' she said. 'I need a real man. And now, thanks to you, I have a chance with Big Bill.' She didn't say her name, so I decided to call her Thump, or Ugh. I decided to stick with the first name – it seemed to fit her better. I watched her turn around and scream down the stairs. 'Bill baby, the dickhead's awake!'

'Cheers, Brittany!' came a voice back, which made me snort with laughter. There was no way this hairy-knuckled woman/bear was called Brittany. I saw her beetle black eyes pierce me as footsteps could be heard on the stairs and Big Bill entered the room. He really was a large fucker. They put on a floor show for me as they kissed as if they were straight out of a cheap porn movie, his large hands matching perfectly her ample attributes.

'Cheers, baby,' he said and gave Brittany's large arse a slap, making her giggle like a schoolgirl. Unfortunately, it sounded more like a cat coughing up a hairball.

'Hey, Bill, so you moved on already?' I said with a smile. 'Such a trooper.' At that point, my nose was put back into place as he back-handed me. It did feel better, albeit briefly.

He grabbed me and my now unfortunately wet chair around to face him as he sat on the bed. We were now face to face, and even with my scar and bloody nose I was still the looker between us.

He stretched and showed off his muscles, which appeared to have muscles on them. I wouldn't say I was intimidated, though anyone in range of sight, smell and on the same plane of existence would see through my lies.

'Now, what's your name, kid?' said Bill.

I raised an eyebrow. 'My name is Tony… *Dad.*' As I spoke that last word, my head shot back as he punched me in the mouth. Clearly, he held it back, though it did make my vision go all swirly.

'Okay, you sparky shit!' he said angrily. 'It's going to end badly for you. Not only did you fuck my wife, but you are treating me with disrespect.'

I coughed a lump of blood up and spat it onto the carpet. I knew that either my life was over, or if I did manage to get away from this place it would never be home like it once was.

'Fair play,' I replied. 'But, in my defence, I didn't know Daphne was your wife, or that you sent her here to check me out.' I could hear the shits downstairs ripping the place apart and eating whatever food I had left.

Bill rubbed his head. 'I can understand that, but at least I got an upgrade.' He gave a sadistic smile. I figured he must be delusional, but I chose not to correct him at this point. 'So, where are the guns?'

I frowned. 'What guns? I've got a couple of shotguns, which you most probably have by now, and the pistol.' I pointed at his waistband, where the gun was still tucked away safely.

'Yeah, that's a nice piece, but I'm talking about a .22 rifle,' he explained with a knowing smile. 'You see, we found bullets in the pockets of one of your jackets. So, I will ask you again. *Where is the rifle?*'

Bugger. 'It was damaged when a horde attacked my last house,' I lied fluently, but it was a crap lie and the man mountain knew it. I could still hear the noise of smashing glass downstairs, but that was another issue as my head was sent backwards again with a punch.

'Bullshit!' said Bill. 'We've seen your recent kills, some pellets, but also some single shots.' His smile had become unfriendly. 'Lie again and see what happens,' he challenged and stared daggers at me. I wondered what would happen if I gave it up? I would be dead, either way.

'I'm not lying,' I said. 'It was destroyed…' That was all I managed to get out as the next punch threw me backwards and, as I was still tied to the chair, that went backwards too. Within seconds, he was on me, landing punch after heavy punch on my face and body, until darkness came to claim me. *Hello, old friend.*

Fair play, he didn't let up the next day, either, though it was mainly shouting. Then he changed his questioning, this time wanting to know if there were any more groups in the surrounding area, and where had I got the tinned food from? It was just like a World War II film with the SS demanding information. Bill didn't like my answers, so he let two of his guys give me a kicking. It wasn't too bad as they kept on getting in each other's way, but once again I was sent away to dreamland. I decided that if the world ever did get back to normal, I would get myself an MRI scan on my head.

This time, I was awoken by the sweet tones of screams. What surprised me was that it wasn't me. Once again, the door was thrown open and a stricken-looking Bill and Thump barrelled through the door. The latter was crying and holding her arm.

'What's going on?' I asked as Bill paced back and forth, while his trophy girlfriend sobbed, with snot and tears streaming. The sound of more screams filtered in through the door. This was starting to panic me some. 'What the fuck is going on?'

'Zombies. It's the fucking zombies, ain't it?' Thump shouted, and I could see blood pumping out from between her fingers.

'WILL YOU TWO STOP TALKING!' Bill shouted angrily as he paced.

I shook my head. 'Didn't you close the gate when you came in?' I said and I saw the blank look. 'You bloody idiots. All this time, I kept it closed and had no bother. You twits turn up and we're all forked!'

Bill walked up to me and pressed the pistol to my head. His whole body was shaking as adrenaline pumped through him. It was then that I saw Brittany starting to convulse on the bed.

'Mate, she's been bitten!' I shouted.

Bill turned his head and his mouth dropped. Then, he raised the gun and killed her in one shot through the side of her head. That brought groans and thumps against the door outside.

'Shit, where's the rifle? We need it,' he demanded, but this time with fear in his voice.

He had no chance and I knew it. 'It's in the barn in the farm across the way,' I said. I flicked my head and that's when I was stuck by his fist again.

'You lying twat!' he yelled and, once again, he put the barrel of the pistol to my head. However, he must have thought twice as the midmorning sun shone into the room. Big Bill walked to the window and smiled. 'Looks like it's time to say goodbye, dickhead.' He then opened the sash window quietly.

'Oh, come on, just let me go,' I begged, albeit in a manly way.

Bill tucked the Luger into the back of his jeans and climbed out onto the window ledge.

'Not a chance,' he said with a vengeful smile on his face. 'Because of you, Daphne and Brittany are dead. So fuck you, Tony.'

'Well, you're going to break your legs jumping out of that window, anyway,' I stated calmly and showed him my ruined smile. 'So I will see you in hell, *buddy*.'

Bill shook his head. 'This is nothing for me. Landing in an overgrown bush is a walk in the park.' He showed me the middle finger. 'Adios, dickhead!' His raised voice caused the zombies on the other side of the door to go mad, and with a wink he was gone.

There was a loud bang and then an 'AAARRRGGHHH!!' Bill's screams flew in through the open window. Well, that didn't sound good. I started to panic and rocked the chair side to side. I had done it before from time to time, when I wasn't being beaten or unconscious, so it was creaking quite nicely. But I wished the big bastard would stop screaming. It was so off putting.

'AAARRRGGHHH!!' it came again.

'WILL YOU SHUT UP! I'M TRYING TO CONCENTRATE!' I screamed back as my chair fell sideways as it collapsed, slamming my punchbag of a head into the floor. *Thank you, thick plush carpeting*. I let out a sob, which the flesh-eating monsters kindly drowned out. I struggled to release my feet, which wasn't too difficult, but I had to slam the arm rest against the wall to get my arms free.

'AAARRRGGHHH!!' came Bill's screams from outside. What a drama queen. What had he done down there? Broken a nail?

By now, the monsters were getting more excited, making the bedroom door flex and creak. I managed to free myself of the last of the zip ties. I then staggered up and went straight to the wardrobe, as I knew the Colonel had left a weapon inside.

'There you are, my pretty,' I said and grabbed the cricket bat. This was some real *Sean of the Dead* shit happening.

I went to the window and looked down. Bill was on the ground, floundering in the bush and screaming like a stuck pig as he tried to drag himself away.

'Hey, buddy, you wanna watch that pistol,' I called down. 'It's not friendly.'

Just then, the bedroom door started to crack and splinter. The bat went out of the window first.

'Heads up… whoops, sorry buddy,' I said as the bat hit Big Bill in the back, and this next bit would stay with me for years.

I leapt from the window and landed on top of Daphne's killer. I was no longer a chubby man, but the ribs I landed on would never be whole again. I presumed Bill had passed out as I stood up and picked grass from my teeth. No, it wasn't a pretty landing. It was like comparing a turkey to a sparrow hawk, and now my bloody knee hurt. Again.

Zombies had begun to pile out of the upstairs window, and let's just say their landings were worse than mine. Also, the noise of Big Bill's screams had attracted the attention of other walkers, who were now appearing from around the side of the house. It was Beefy Botham time. I reclaimed the cricket bat and started to swing. The trouble was, they kept on coming.

But it was Big Bill who inadvertently saved my life. He finally came to and began to scream again, which surprised me. I thought I had destroyed his chest cavity when I landed on him. However, the noise drew every zombie's eye and they began to move towards him. At that moment, I disappeared stage right, leaping like a young gazelle, trying to keep my trailing leg from catching the fence. But this gazelle caught his front foot and I was sent flying onto the sodden ground, face first. This turned out to be fortunate because the zombies that weren't feeding on Big Bad Bill looked for me, and as I had seemed to have disappeared from sight under my camouflage, they joined in with pulling the Happy Meal apart rather than pursuing me.

Bill's cries died quite quickly as I commando crawled across the rotten crops. You couldn't even call them crops, as they were more like mush now. With a look over my shoulder, I jumped up and began to run as if my life depended on it. With a pop my knee screamed and, once again, I had a face full of mulch. It took a whole hour for me to make my escape. Clearly, that should be a very sad record somewhere.

I made it to the gun store and grabbed the much-coveted rifle before slowly limping down to the farm's gate; the chain and lock were still there, so I put them to good use and secured the gate before heading back up to the adjoining field. The garden was packed and clearly Bill was now gone. A couple of zombies had fallen over the fence into the field, but they would be dealt with soon enough as they were trying to rejoin the horde and not chew on me.

It had been a busy couple of days and my face – in fact, everything – hurt. So I let myself into the farmhouse, found a comfy bed and, with a bottle of water in hand, I slept my pain away, almost.

I settled in the farm for a good couple of days as the horde finished their work. The thugs that turned and had caused so much death and destruction had put up a fight, but not enough to hold back the tide of zombies that they had brought upon themselves.

It had gone wrong so fast. Why couldn't we have just lived together? But that's what life is in the Zombie Apocalypse. I was thankful for my forward thinking of placing food and water stashes in surrounding homes. Never thought I would ever get to say that about myself, but of course nobody was here to see me being this dynamic apocalyptic warrior.

Finally, on the third day, I deemed it safe enough to venture out and slowly crept across the sodden field that was the barrier between the two properties. Clearly, some carrion had been enjoying themselves on those poor bastards who had fallen outside my once home. It truly was party time if you were a crow or cousin.

The Colonel's house was a mess. Mud, blood and flesh littered the place. Some of the zombies' victims had resurrected. However, as there was hardly anything left but bones and their heads, they just lay on the ground and groaned the song of their people. With a soft crack of my rifle, each one was sent into the afterlife for judgement. After that, I decided to move residency to the farm next door.

I found my stash of painkillers and anti-inflammatories and threw them in the bag with anything else of use, which wasn't much as either the idiots or the walkers had destroyed everything. I could reclaim foodstuffs and water from the other safe houses and bring them all back to the farm before deciding on my next plan of action. It was still fairly cold at night, so I used the vehicles I requisitioned to transport the gas cylinder back to the farm. That way, at least I could be warm, especially as the horde had now moved on.

The gang's vehicles were on their last legs as it was. I read somewhere that the additive they put in petrol only lasted a finite amount of time. I figured that must be it. Look at me, using the word finite. At least for the next month I had a place to live and time to decide on a plan of action. But where to go? Cities were a no go.

As the nights passed, I read a few of the farmer's wife's romance books. One was about some barrel-chested horse trainer called Diego Montoya, who made love to many a lonely housewife in a stable, leaving broken hearts and families in his wake. I looked at the book cover.

'What a load of bollocks,' I muttered and sent it flying into the deepest and dirtiest corner of the house. I mused about a story of my own life – 'Tony the Terrible' and the night of passion with a tattooed traveller. Yep, a 99p e-book if I ever did see one.

With the milder spring weather now drawing in, I found that the game birds I had shot had a shorter hanging life. That meant I had to hunt every day, which would mean a lot more bullets or shells would be required for the shotgun. Also, the game itself would be on the move; for some strange reason, they didn't wish to die in order to keep me alive. Who would have thought nature could be so selfish?

The time had come for me to finally move on. It was either leave or starve to death. Especially as I was now on my last roll of toilet paper – it was as if I was living in the middle ages. I gathered my water and some tins of food. As I packed my bag, the weight was starting to build. Yes, I could take a car, but in this dead, noiseless world, everyone and their zombie neighbours would hear me. I had survived the hordes so far, but I didn't want to push my luck any more than I needed to.

To keep down the weight, I chose to take just the rifle, the newest shotgun and the trusty and blood-smeared cricket bat. It was a risk, but I dismantled the shotgun and, just like I had seen in the movies, I cut it down with a metal saw. I left the shoulder stock, but cut the barrels down to just in front of the foregrip. That meant that I could carry it in my rucksack. The gun would also be empty – I had no desire to leave my backside behind.

I decided I would leave in the morning and walk cross-country, moving from house to house, hoping to find some food and company. I might even find safety in one of the towns. I needed some road signs and a map. And possibly someone to read said map, as I knew at some point

I'd need to follow a road or two. When the moronic Bill had turned up, he had changed my mind instantly about travelling by car. Yes, you need people to survive, but they had to be the right people. So I would keep hidden and watch those I find. It was now pissing down, so I sat indoors and watched the gutters overflowing with water. Spring in England. Nothing finer.

Chapter 11

After two days, the weather broke and some dry, but cloudy, sky had taken over from his moody brother, Mr Rainy, who seemed to like to piss on my world. I threw my rucksack onto my back and tightened the straps over the farmer's wax jacket I had found in a shed. After all, it was spring, which meant that in two minutes' time it could be pissing it down.

I slipped the cricket bat between the bag and my back. It rubbed a bit, but I would just have to see how long I would be able to tolerate it before launching it into the trees. It was either the bat or the rifle. Somehow, I felt safer with the gun. Go figure. I climbed over the fence at the back of the property and headed in a hitherto untravelled direction. Thirty minutes into my journey, I was back at the farm to pick up my shotgun ammo belt and the last box of .22 bullets, which I had left on the kitchen table. Then, once again, I headed off with swear words being muttered under my breath. Second time lucky, I guess.

As I walked through the sodden English countryside, I stopped again to move the bat and put it into the backpack. It just proved what a novice apocalyptic warrior I was. For the last few days, I had tried to find a map, but without luck. Unless, of course, it was one of Iraq and Afghanistan – that was the Colonel's, by the way. I didn't think the farmer and his family were much for travelling.

The trouble was, I didn't know where I was. My mind had been focused on escaping my home town alive. Not only that, but I hadn't checked any bills or personal letters at any of the properties I had been in. Let's just face it, my survival skills were balls.

I passed several houses on my walk, though. Unfortunately, zombies were still about, but the best moment was finding a badly mangled car that had had a head-on argument with a very large, old and immovable tree. There was barely anything left of what you could call a body, which I presumed to be the driver and who had been stopped quite forcefully by said tree. The plus point was the bottle of unopened water and a road map.

'Score!'

The run-in with Big Bill had caused me to be wary, so I kept off the roads. Instead, I walked over adjoining fields. If any traffic did come along, I had time to hide so I wouldn't be spirited away and become someone's love slave. Let's face it, we all know that's what will end up happening to my now firm ass. I wondered if Olga was still alive.

By now, the light had started to fade, and I knew I hadn't made much progress. But then again, there was no schedule and, if I didn't die, I'd be winning. I came upon a small bungalow. It was standing on a large patch of ground, the neighbours being at least a quarter of a mile down the road. Luckily, the field I was in ran around it, so I crouched down and hid behind the stone wall, moving slowly around the perimeter. The curtains were open, the lawn was overgrown (shocker) and I couldn't see any movement. My trousers were getting soaked in the long grass as

I moved. It was then that I could see a body on the grey stone-covered driveway. Also on the driveway was a Mini. It had blood-smeared windows and the driver's door was open. What was once a person was underneath the car. Not sure what the story was, but it had obviously been played out months ago.

I jumped over the wall with only a slight twinge from my knee, though it might have been down to the weight in my rucksack. Next time, I would leave it behind and reclaim it once I had cleared the property. The front door was locked, as was the kitchen door. However, the gods of safety and patio doors were shining on me once again.

I slipped off my bag and placed the rifle alongside the coiled-up green garden hose that was attached to the garden wall. My knee grumbled as I knelt and dug through my pack, pulling out the unloaded sawn-off shotgun. I broke it open and slipped a couple of cartridges into the breach and, with a snap, I was ready to head in. Clueless as I was, I did know that this was the perfect weapon for enclosed spaces. So, with the stock in my shoulder, I moved to the door.

With my breathing calmed, I walked slowly to the patio door and placed my left hand on the handle, slowly opening the door all the way. The PVC door didn't make a sound as it swung open. My eyes flitted around. The house was a mess and I could see multiple bloody handprints on the wall. I flicked off the safety catch with my thumb.

The living room was clear, as was the kitchen. My feet were quiet on the carpet, which helped as I headed deeper into the bungalow. I stilled as I saw a pair of legs splayed out at the end of the hall and, with my gun raised, I continued slowly. Then I saw the owner of the legs – zombie grandma, wearing a dusty blue dress. She was just sitting there, glassy eyed. Her hands were torn and bloody and I could see the reason; she had been beating on a closed door for some time. But why?

I cleared my throat, which instantly got a reaction from the blue-haired woman. I aimed quickly and, with one ear-shattering, head-splattering headshot, it brought the way too familiar splatter pattern up the wall, with my gun up and smoking from a barrel. I waited for any other movements; it took a while for my ears to stop ringing. Then, in total silence, I moved from door to door. The place screamed retirement. Hopefully, there would be some food for me to eat while I worked out my plan.

What lay behind the bloodied door that the zombie had been eager to gain entry to would normally have broken my heart. I had to barge my way in. Some cheap, white, put-together furniture had been piled up behind the door, but it was easy for me to push past, revealing a truly sad sight. I presumed that the grandson had come to visit his grandma, either in the Mini or was driven by another, but the boy had managed to flee to safety in this room. For some reason, however, he chose never to leave it again. The blond-haired teenager had decayed to the point of being no more than bones wrapped in leather-like skin. Though all the signs were still there of what he once was and how he'd done the deed, the knife and the note told me all. So I dragged his nan into the room to be with him and closed the door with a click of its lock.

There were some tins of food in the cupboards and a packet of rice, along with a few litre bottles of water, which was handy. There wasn't a fireplace, but there was a wood burner with a good deal of compressed woodchip logs by the side. And so, after a few hours of frustration trying to lodge a saucepan in the burner, I finally managed to cook a bowl of rice mixed with a can of plum tomatoes. It was nothing fancy, but it was hot and tasty.

Despite my desire to move, I decided to stay at the bungalow until I had used everything they had. There were still a few shufflers moving up and down the road, which I imagined were brought forth due to the gunshot. But the bungalow was locked and secure, and I had heat and food for a good few days. That meant I could relax on the sofas in safety as I scoured the map. I decided to head towards Aylesbury, a large town surrounded by small villages and fields, which was perfect. Although I had found travelling via the fields tiring and wetter than roads, it did seem that zombies were not the rambling type. They preferred open roads to ploughed fields.

The downside of being British was the lack of guns and ammo. Had I been in America, I would have an M1 Abrams tank already with a 50-calibre machine chain gun sat upon it (thank you, Modern Warfare Game). Apart from the occasional weapons I found in neighbouring farms, finding ammo was getting worrisome. I had only what I had brought with me.

After exhausting the food supply in the grandmother's bungalow, I headed back into the fields. It was slow-going, the rifle was out and the unloaded shotgun was tucked away. It was hard work, but the first day allowed me to pick off a cock pheasant, who was happy to stand still long enough for me to send it to game bird heaven. I walked as I plucked, leaving feathers in my wake.

Once again, things worked out well for me, as a cottage with a 'For sale' sign appeared in front of me. I dropped my rucksack and pheasant at the fence line and climbed over into the garden. It was all secure apart from the front door, which was wide open with a suitcase wedging the door open. In the driveway sat a dirty car with the boot wide open and suitcases, boxes of water and food stuffed in it. It was covered in grime, so clearly it had been open to the elements for a fair while. However, the food was sealed, so hopefully it would still be edible.

I ran back to the fence to collect my bag and pheasant, then brought both items back and swapped the guns around before loading them and heading inside. It was totally clear. When I saw the sale sign, I was initially worried that the property would be devoid of all home comforts, but I was wrong. It was all here – just musty and a little damp. The plus point was the wood burning stove and the open fire.

'Tony will be fed and warm again, tonight,' I muttered as I finished the house check.

When I looked out of the front bedroom window, the view down into the large paved, but overgrown, driveway gave me an outline of what happened that fateful day.

By the looks of the house, it had belonged to a youngish couple, no kids, and they had loaded up the car together. What looked like the young wife had been attacked while trying to get into the driver's door. That's where her devoured corpse now lay, still wearing her little black pixie boots. The husband was over in the rose bushes and still trying to extract himself from them. Clearly, the wife's brain had been damaged in her passing.

I walked down to the kitchen and found a golf club in an umbrella stand. I allowed a smile to creep across my face as I grabbed it and headed towards what I presumed was the zombie husband.

'YOU MOTHER FUCKER!!' I screamed and swung my hardest at the zombie, who was now on all fours. With a dull thump, he dropped, but I didn't stop there. I went to town on the poor bugger. At least he was with his wife now – unless it wasn't him, then tough titties. I left the club still attached to him and walked away before starting to empty the car, undoing all their hard work.

That night, I sat on a comfy sofa with the doors locked, shutting the murderous world out. The smell of roast pheasant filtered through the house as the open fire started to banish the musty smell of a damp, but once happy, home. At this moment in time, with a bottle of beer warming my belly, I was truly happy. It was just the loneliness that was starting to become a burden to me.

The former owners had some good books that lightened my mood, so I spent a week there drying my clothes out and claiming some spoils as my own. A new pack of pants was a godsend, as mine were starting to fight back, so I laid those to rest in the fire.

'Goodbye, old friends. You served me well,' I said in the candlelit night.

After my stay there, I headed out once again into the English countryside with clean pants, a few new books to read at night, and a song in my heart. There was hope today as the spring sun turned up before the rain did. For the next four days, I trudged through mud and grass for hours on end, checking houses for anything that I needed. I found some .22 ammo, another hundred cartridges for the shotgun, bottles of water, sugary drinks and tins of food. Not to mention a family-size bag of pickled onion Monster Munch (winner).

The cost for all that was me hurting my knee again after going all commando, leaping over a stone wall and ending up in the fetal position, crying for my long dead mummy. However, after almost overdosing on painkillers and ibuprofen, I was good to go again following a solid eight hours of fluid-leaking unconsciousness. Apart from that, I killed ten zombies of mixed gender, race and region. No racism or sexism here. Oh, and I killed a parrot who screamed in my ear as I walked into his house. The latter tasted quite nice.

And that was how I spent the rest of the week, chilling out in a home which was once owned by some crazy bastard who enjoyed chopsy parrots. I looked at the map and smiled as I saw the next challenge en route to what I hoped was salvation. Aylesbury!

Chapter 12

'What in the ever-loving Mad Max fuck is going on here?' I said quietly to myself. It took me another whole week of walking and house checking, but finally I had made it to a place that had been pointed out to me on many car trips of my youth. The country home of the prime minister of the United Kingdom – whoever that is or was, as by now I couldn't remember. I'm not sure why, but I had Donald Trump in my head, but I was pretty sure it was the Yanks who had voted in that gem.

This large mansion was set in the midst of some of the UK's most stunning countryside, where dignitaries from all around the world were wined and dined while being treated to the finest cuisine possible. Yeah, but that's not what I saw. First thing I found was where the zombie horde had been spending most of its time. Yep, surrounding the prime minister's surprisingly fortified compound. Before, it had just a normal wall which was most probably guarded by the best troops in the land. Now, though, it was a bit different.

I settled into my new, yet temporary, home. It was comprised of a group of shrubs on the edge of some woods that surrounded one side of the now dangerous compound, but it allowed me to hide while monitoring the goings on during the daylight hours. When I had decided to come here, I had a couple of thoughts. Firstly, I had presumed it would be a burnt-out husk, with nothing left to speak of or worth stealing. My other thought was that the PM would be in situ surrounded by the full might of the armed forces – SAS, Paras, Marines, Commandos, even the bloody Salvation Army – and they would invite any lone apocalyptic wanderer in to feast and drink heartily and I could finally live out my life with Olga, if she was still alive and liked me that way.

That was what I was expecting. In front of me, however, was everything that was wrong with the new world. The only positive spin was that the grass of the compound was perfect. The downside was the Mad Max-style thugs riding on dirt bikes around what appeared to be slaves cutting the grass. There were guards everywhere walking around in black police uniforms or army camo gear. But the sight that disturbed me the most, as I looked through my binoculars, was the people who had been crucified. Unfortunately, the magnified images showed me that the victims weren't tied to the crosses; instead, they had been nailed through their palms and feet. What the hell.

Had I been in my right mind I would have run, screaming all the way back to the little bungalow I had been staying in since I'd arrived in the nearby village, then packed up and carried on running until I hit France. I didn't know how my inquisitive mind had gotten the better of me, damn and blast him to hell… twice.

It was on the third day, still in my hideout and watching, that I saw something else that truly did disgust me. The slaves were gathered into a group facing a stage built at the front of the old manor house. The guards were circling them, while giving the odd slave a jab from their rifle butts to keep them in line.

Suddenly, applause rippled through the group, which riled up the zombies surrounding their compound. Then, as I watched through my binoculars, I could see what the excitement was all about. A large, bald man appeared, with muscles that even I could see were huge. Not only that, but on his arm was a tall, slender model of a woman. Her long, blonde hair reached down to her waist and she sported a haughty look.

The big man stepped forward with his arms wide open. As he began to speak, his baritone voice echoed over the land. I figured he must have really loved the sound of his own voice.

'My friends, what a fine job you have been doing in service of me and my troops this past week,' he boomed in his strong Welsh accent. I wondered whether he and his choir had invaded England for the sunny climate and to get away from the cold Welsh weather in the west. 'But, as always, there are some who chose to swim against the tide, wishing not to do their bit to keep us fed and safe. They abused my trust and your loyalty...'

I watched as two men and one women were dragged out in front of the crowd, all bloody and beaten.

'Shit, that doesn't bode well,' I said softly just as the wind started to pick up, as if it knew what was about to happen and opposed it.

'They stole food and drink from houses in my domain,' continued the man, 'which takes food off of your plates.' He shouted to his masses, smiling at them. I half expected him to break out into song about mining or sheep, but there were grumbles coming from the group.

However, with the help of some well-aimed rifle butts, that soon stopped.

'At this time tomorrow, these trespassers will be put to death as a statement to all those who think they have rights over my lands…' He raised his chin imperiously. 'Now, back to work my friends. After all, it is a nice day.'

'HAIL KING JONES! ALL HAIL KING JONES!' the masses chanted. That did make me bark out a laugh. After all these years, the Welsh had finally invaded England to within a stone's throw away from the capital. What a strange, scary world we now lived in.

As I scanned the crowd and the walls with the binoculars, I did wonder how the slaves managed to get out of the compound to forage, especially as the horde was always surrounding them – from what I could see, anyway.

By now, darkness was beginning to fall over the land. Once the sun had gone down, it became quite chilly, forcing me to light a fire. Hopefully the little cottage I slept in was far enough away from the compound for them to see the smoke.

With a can of spaghetti bolognaise simmering on a small camping stove, thoughts about what I had seen plagued me, and I began wondering what I could do to help those poor sods. What worried me was that, if I was caught, my fate would be the death penalty. But I had to do something. I was no longer that marshmallow body of an online gamer and recluse. I was now a seasoned killer of zombie and man alike, whether I wanted to be or not. I would save these people. And, as sleep overtook me later that evening, my mind planned for the coming day.

As the sun rose, I readied myself. Obviously, I wouldn't be able to stay here if I went through with the plan, so I packed up all my stuff and hoisted my rucksack and headed out into the morning sun. I found a cottage that sat what I deemed within range of my target – not quite straight on, but close enough. I set myself up in the front bedroom that had a view of the manor. I sat on my rucksack, then gently opened the window, just enough so I could poke the rifle out and scan the area with the scope. It was a long shot, but I was hopeful.

Thinking back to all the war films I had seen in the good and happy years, I remembered that I needed something with which to gauge the wind. And there it was, the Welsh national flag snapping in the early morning breeze. I smiled, as the shot would be face on and so I should have a bigger target. Plus, King John was a big unit, anyway. His so-called subjects were already at work tending the lawns. It was then that I saw the chickens running around the place, and the calls of other animals. I decided that they must have a few animals for butchering. They had everything and it looked like that bald Welshman would do anything to keep it.

Luckily, I had some dried fruit and water to keep me going as I watched the camp bustling away. I felt for the poor shits inside; it resembled one of those Nazi workcamps, but with inmates wearing tracksuits and torn uniforms. As the time ticked by, there seemed to be more of an urgency to their movements. The guards were herding the slaves towards the front of the manor again. Then I saw the three condemned people being led to the front and forced to kneel down with their hands bound behind their backs. The woman was clearly sobbing. I could see, even from this distance, her dirty blonde hair flying in the breeze.

Soon enough, the applause filtered through the crowd as the King, as he liked to be called, strode out of the manor once again, this time wearing a gaudy jewel-encrusted crown. The stroppy tall blonde was on his arm again, this time in a long white ball gown, and what appeared to be a tiara which glistened in the sunlight. I moved the scope to the flag and saw it flapping, but not too much. I had confidence in my ability. I moved my sights down and settled on the head of the King, using the large gem that nestled on the front of his crown as the target. He had his woman and a few others sitting on ornate polished wooden chairs as he went through his spiel. Boy, did he love the sound of his own voice.

I moved the crosshairs down towards the man's large chest and slowed my breathing. Taking a life is never easy, and it shouldn't be. But seeing a meat cleaver sitting upon a red velvet-looking cushion, which a young boy was holding at the back of the stage, made it a little easier somehow. The safety catch was clicked off. My breathing was steady, though my heart was hammering away like a woodpecker on speed.

The man was ranting now, shouting at the crowds. He beckoned towards the nervous boy who held the weapon-adorned cushion, and the boy slowly moved closer, visibly shaking.

Crack!

As usual, there was little to no recoil on the small calibre rifle. Unseen to the human eyes, the projectile span itself towards its target in the divine hope that it would cast away another blight on this beautiful land. And it should've happened, as I was a good shot. But no, nothing happened.

Thanks to his rants and the groans of Thriller video rejects that surrounded the manor, the shot was never heard. As I reloaded and the scope moved around, that's when I noticed a man sitting at the back looking around; and that's when I saw a pale spot on the wall over the man's shoulder. It seemed the first shot had veered to the right, missing the King and almost killing a random man who looked like David Baddiel. But I did manage to damage the mansion, so at least that was something. Take that, fucker.

So, once again, like the pro I was pretending to be, I adjusted the telescopic sight and took aim at the man's barrel-like chest. He was now waving the cleaver around. My breathing settled as he stood over the sobbing woman and rose the shiny death bringer to the heavens, where I'm guessing it was unwanted, unless St Michael the Archangel was about to swoop down to smite the unworthy with his mighty flaming chopper.

Anyway, I sent another one of the small bullets flying towards the possible mass murderer and felt my ticket to heaven being reserved. The large man fell backwards onto his once prim and proper queen, as screams and shouts echoed around the ground as what appeared to be the royal family gathered around the now flailing queen.

The air stilled as the huge man began to move. He sat up and it felt as though his small, piggy eyes were tearing into my soul. He lifted a meaty paw to his head and it came away bloody.

'FUUUCKKK!' I said loudly as the man's bloodied finger pointed towards me. God only knew how he could see me. And that's when the window exploded inwards, showering me in glass. With my need to pee suspiciously disappearing, I dropped to the ground and threw my bag though the door and followed it in a very awkward commando crawl, trying to drag the rifle with me. The rain of glass had stopped, having been replaced by wood and brick dust.

With my bag on my back and rifle in hand, I burst out of the cottage as if the hounds of hell were after me. Unfortunately, that description was quite accurate, as the sound of high-pitched motorcycle engines came filtering my way. How the hell they got there without being torn to pieces was beyond me. I was running down the road, though I knew that would soon come to an end as my body was starting to fall to pieces. I was sure they could hear the creaking of my knee, the wheezing of my lungs, or most probably the slapping of my flat feet on tarmac.

Woods, here I come. And, like a sprightly stag, I jumped into the shadow-ridden woods, bracken and branches cracking underfoot. The motorbikes were still heading up the road in an effort to catch me up, and they were coming fast, so I sat down behind a large tree with my rifle at my shoulder. I moved the gun around the side of my wooden shield, causing flakes of the old bark to drop to the ground. I looked down the gun sights, scanning the area, when three dirt bikes appeared at full pelt, black smoke pluming from the exhausts into the clean air.

I shook my head while musing about what would happen if they caught me. They did seem quite passionate about wanting to get to know me. My internal dialogue stopped as the hunters carried on by. It wouldn't be long before the deadheads followed them. Why wouldn't they? Those bikes were as noisy as hell. But maybe that was their plan? They were using zombies to flush me out?

'Bugger,' I muttered. It was a good plan, too, and if they did catch me they would match the empty shells to my rifle.

The wood thickened as the path I was following started to disappear. It must have been a deer track or something. Who was I kidding? I didn't know what had caused the trail to be made. All I knew was that I was lost and making too much damned noise, so I slowed my pace and picked my way through the foliage.

The bikes now sounded like nothing more than angry wasps in the air, which filled me with hope. Maybe, just maybe, I had gotten away with it. My now clicking knee was hurting me even more, forcing me to use the last of my painkillers, which would mean my pace would become even slower. I sat on an old moss-covered tree stump, waiting as I let the medicine do its work, when the sound of rustling in the trees made me instantly raise my weapon again, showing anyone who cared to watch how twitchy I had become. However, all I could see was a brace of grey squirrels playing grab ass in the canopy of trees. It did bring a smile to my face as I watched them having so much fun, and for a moment it took me back to my childhood and betters times.

Chapter 13

The woods were silent once again. I guessed the bushy-tailed animals were busy trying to bury their nuts or hiding their food somewhere safe to survive the oncoming winter. This brought me to wondering if I would ever reach somewhere safe again, and a manly tear ran down my grime-covered cheek.

The drugs had given me a lovely buzz, so I felt it was time to carry on my journey to safety and a comfy toilet. I would give my throne for a porcelain one. After another hour of stalking through the trees, I saw the outline of another village, which pleased me, especially as I hadn't heard the bikes in at least three quarters of an hour. I wasn't sure how I came up with that estimation of time. So, touch wood, they had either given up or were just chasing something or someone else.

I moved to a broken garden gate which led to the now typical scene of an overgrown garden. However, this two-storey house had a child's climbing frame as well as a rusted swing. I knelt down in the long grass behind an old stone bird bath, even though my knee screamed for rest, but I focused and kept my breathing shallow as I listened for any sign of life. Unfortunately, being that close to the wood made it difficult, as it seemed like every wood pigeon in England was serenading me. I put the rifle sling over my head, brought out the shortened shotgun, and placed two cartridges into the breach, snapping it closed. I then began to move forward, looking through each window. There was nothing. I clicked off the safety catch as I saw the back door was open. Rotten leaves had blown in during the autumn/winter and had made this tomb of a house their home.

The fact that the leaves were still stuck to the floor meant it hadn't seen any humans, alive or dead, in a long while. I closed the door and headed deeper into the house. The front door stood wide open, the glass cracked across both panes. Just as many people had done every day of their short lives, I closed it for possibly its final time. Dramatic, eh? I carried on my journey through the property. The two bedrooms were empty – just bare bed frames, nothing more. The bathroom was devoid of anything useful from the garish pink bathroom suite, but needs must so a clogging movement was dropped into the bone dry bowl.

The wet wipes topped off my gift, but before leaving I opened the window, just in case I decided to stay here for the night or more. However, a diet of power bars and chocolate does not make for a good diet. Closing the bathroom door, I moved to the front bedroom and scanned the area from the window. The house was situated in a small cul-de-sac with four domiciles in a circle, all with doors open and rubbish strewn across their front lawns. As I physically relaxed my body, my weak joint started to thrum with pain and stiffness, so I decided to make this house my home for the night.

Using a wall as a pillow, I sat down and allowed my senses to close down as tiredness overcame me, and I fell into darkness and bad dreams. A noise like a chainsaw invaded my dreams, where Olga was willingly trying on her new uniform. The noise grew louder as a man, who looked like the King, walked in carrying a running chainsaw.

'Oh, shit... Mummy!' I cried out, making me jump and all of my muscles joined me in the cry. It was pitch black, but a light was illuminating the house. I poked my head above the dust-encrusted windowsill and saw what was causing the light and sound; one of the dirt bikes was slowly moving down the road. The rider didn't seem to know I was here, as he coasted back out of the road and headed off in a boom of noise. How brazen they were.

Sleep came easy enough for me again. This time there were no dreams, just a blanket of nothingness. I was awoken by the sun's rays, seemingly magnified through the bedroom window, and starting to burn holes through my eyelids. Okay, maybe I might stretch the truth, but it bloody hurt. After a few minutes of complaining and general bitching, I crawled to the bathroom and added to the toilet's woes. I sat there and looked through an out-of-date Argos catalogue and I was amazed by its lack of zombie-killing implements for the general public. After all, we weren't allowed to buy guns willingly, so you would have thought the said store would've been stocked with machetes, baseball bats with designer nails added to the ends, name of bats to be agreed on at time of purchase. Now, however, it was all boring.

The wet wipes fought their battle and, once again, they were victorious and rested on top of the pile. It was now time for me to flee this now oddly smelling abode. That's when I started to notice the moans and groans, and it wasn't some young couple exercising their rights for free love. I ran to the window and saw the zombies shuffling down the road.

'FUCKKKK,' I said out loud as there were way too many. Like a river, they washed over the road and went into every house that was open, flowing around the parked cars. They were unstoppable. My last chance of escape was the back door. I packed my rucksack and left a pair of war-torn pants behind for future beings to wonder what had happened to me.

'Damn it to merry hell!' I cursed as the zombies seemed to know where I was and were gathering around the front and back doors. I could hear the glass on both doors cracking, bit by bit, as the zombies pushed to get to the tasty morsel, which was me. I headed back upstairs and leant out of the front window and a had a look around. There, in the distance, sat a 4x4 and my three biker friends, who were clearly happy to see me, as they were all sporting a creepy smile. Hopefully, tonight was not date night.

I quickly went into the back bedroom and looked out the window. A small group of the undead were in the garden, but they were having difficulty moving because of the long grass. As my mind raced, the sound of cracking of glass downstairs increased and the moans and groans of the zombies become louder with every passing second. The sun was beating down now, causing beads of sweat to appear on my face, while thoughts of my impending death did not help matters. I could see the swing and the climbing frame sticking out from the long grass, but they were too far away. The neighbour's fence was not even close and I had no way to get there.

Insanity came knocking at that moment. Under the grass, only five foot away from the house, I could see a possible way out, or a tragically painful death. A small trampoline, hidden by the long grass, but vaguely discernible from my vantage point. I decided it needed to be tested. So, keeping hold of my shotgun, I lodged the cricket bat and rifle into the rucksack and I aimed. Then I launched the bag out into the warm sunshine, watching it plummet down into the grass and then bounce over the neighbour's fence. It worked for the bag, but could it work for this hunk of man muscle? I was in two minds as I sat on the windowsill with my feet planted on the alarm box, which the last owners had added for their family's safety. Clearly, this wasn't what they had in mind when they bought it.

The noise downstairs was getting worse. Not only that, but the sound of engines could be heard along with some gunfire. I dreaded to think what they were doing. Now, should I land feet first and hope the trampoline wouldn't give out, fall through and shatter my legs? Or land on my back and hope the foliage would lessen the fall? The decision was made for me as one of the glass doors shattered. I made sure the gun had the safety catch on and I let fly.

As the wind whistled past my ears, I could hear R. Kelly singing to me about flying. The trampoline held and, instead of pain, I felt elation as, once again, my recently abused body took flight. But that's when it went a bit Pete Tong (wrong). When I landed on the trampoline, I didn't go straight up. Instead, I went off to the side, and that's when darkness hit me once again.

Laughter, that's what I awoke to. That and gunfire, as I heard the dead that had been all around, their noises growing less and less as the gunfire rolled on. Then there was silence, all except for the laughter. Faces came into view.

'Hey, dickhead, that was the funniest thing I ever saw!' mocked a man with a beard and no front teeth. 'But the King wants to see ya!' He raised my shotgun and slammed the stock into my head, sending me back to sleep... Ow.

I could feel movement and noise. I guessed I had been placed into the back of the 4x4 for transit. Although my body ached like I had been massaged with a hammer, I decided to keep my eyes and mouth closed, despite my past history of gobbing off. I listened to the men in front talking. It was difficult, but I managed to catch a few bits of gossip... King pissed (shocker). Funniest thing ever, trampoline, face first into a fence... That explained why my face hurt. And so, with that little titbit of knowledge, my pride was now as bruised as my body – though it was not the first time that this bad boy had taken a kicking.

Some gates were opened and my carriage drove me to my fate, whatever it may be. And all because those people decided my home was theirs on that fateful day. May they rot in hell. Gravity aided me out of the back of the truck, making me emit a groan of pain as I hit the concrete.

'Well, looky here. Old Eddie the Eagle is awake,' said a man with a gravelly voice. 'Grab his legs and drag him to cell three. The King wants him healthy.' There then came mocking laughter as my poor, bruised body was dragged down some steps. The back of my head kept count of how many steps there were; the final count was difficult, but by my fuzzy mind told me twelve.

Finally, I allowed myself to open my eyes and view my new home. I appeared to be in what looked like old-fashioned stables, with iron bars and locks on the doors and straw scattered on the floor. There was a cough from the other side of the wooden wall.

'Hello? Anyone there?' I called out.

'Shhh! Not so loud, they'll hear,' came a hushed voice. I managed to get up and limp to the other wall before my body gave out and wilted, slamming my sore back into the wood. 'Are you Eddie?'

I rolled my eyes, but even that small movement made me wince with pain. How the hell can you strain your eyes? Unless you're engaging in conversation with a lady of certain proportions, and you are doing your best to keep eye contact only.

'No, my name is Tony, Tony Anderson,' I answered and hoped they would put the whole Eddie the Eagle thing to rest soon.

'Watchya, Tony,' replied the voice. 'Why are they calling you the other name, then?' Another muffled one said something, which I couldn't quite grasp. 'Anyway, where are my manners? My name is Jim Stone, and my twin brother is John.'

'Hi, so what did you do to get locked up?' I asked. I realised the voice was coming from a small knothole in one of the wooden planks that looked like they had seen a few things, and possibly not good things, either.

'Nothing,' replied Jim in a London twang. 'We were just scavenging from house to house, and trying to survive just like anyone else. They wanted us to join their workforce, but we declined their offer.' He then had a muffled conversation with his brother. 'Well, I told them to fuck off,' continued Jim. 'So, was it you who tried to off the big man?'

How many films had I seen where they tell you to plead innocent, and never trust anyone who has something to gain from dobbing you in?

'No,' I replied. 'I just got caught while having a kip in a house. Who's this big man, then?' I asked, acting my heart out. *Thank you for your nominations – and, of course, the Academy Award*

Jim barked out a laugh. 'He's just some taffy, thinks he's their King or summit. What I heard, he's really pissed as a bullet split his scalp open, and his workforce are calling him the Jap's Eye now. He ain't happy!' Jim laughed even harder.

I rubbed the back of my head and my hand came away covered in sticky blood. It did make me wonder why I ever left my flat. Apart from fire, starvation and zombies, it had been fine.

'I wonder if they will believe me if I said I didn't do it, mate?' I stated and the twins gave a dark laugh, one slightly more muffled than the other one.

'Nah, they seem to be more of the "act now and can't be bothered to ask questions later" type of crowd,' Jim said and whispered to his brother. 'They were going to throw us to the dead today, but I guess old Jap's Eye had other things on his mind – mainly you, Tony!'

I had no idea if they'd found my rucksack or rifle. I wondered whether I would simply be thrown to the zombies – which, between that and having my head cut off, seemed the lesser of the two evils. If I'd had a working body, I might have been able to wriggle past the meat eaters.

'Sounds like I'm fucked then, mate,' I said and shifted my weight to be more comfortable, which made me groan like an old man.

A muffled sound could be heard. 'Ain't that right?' said Jim. 'John says we're all fucked, anyway. Even if we could get out of this cell, we are zombie bait. And that's all of us, mate.'

Just then, the large door to the building was kicked open.

'EDDIE THE EAGLE, YOUR PUBLIC AWAITS!' boomed a voice.

I really hoped that the real Eddie had messed up and had landed here, too. The door opened and there stood two, huge-bellied and bearded men wearing combat gear. But even the best camouflage in the world would struggle to hide their fat arses. I stared at them and wished I could do a runner. *I think I could beat them… just… downhill… possibly.*

I tried to give them the best smile I had in my charm locker and delved deep into my mind for the perfect greeting to these two man-mountains and gift to blind women everywhere. Then it came to me like a bolt of divine lighting. The words were on the tip of my tongue. All the little people who dwell in my brain, who have cheered and talked me into many adventures in the past – would they fail me now? I doubted it.

'Hey, slims, who's gonna do the truffle shuffle for me, then?' I said, sporting a big toothy grin. I heard a chuckle from the cell next door before it started to rain fists, and once again I was introduced into the realms of unconsciousness. I would really need a scan on my brain when the world was right again.

I am woken up into a world of laughter. My hearing was the first of my senses to begin working, and then my vision came into play. My eyes began to flutter like a teen girl trying to attract a special companion. As the blurring began to recede, it was then I saw the huge Welshman known as the King – or, as the twins had explained to me, John Jones from Pontypridd in Wales. He had once been a semi-professional rugby player until some big Brit shattered his knee in a local club game, which had left him on the nasty side of temperate.

'Well, well, looks like Eddie is awake,' the bald-headed king joked. My eyes were fixed on the bandage wrapped around his head, which made me smirk internally. The men were still laughing. 'Wish I could've seen him flying, face first, into that fence. What a stupid twat!'

This was really starting to piss me off. Like they had the balls to leap from a first-floor window onto a trampoline, and it hadn't even been the first time I'd done it. Last time, I didn't even use a trampoline – I used Big Bill.

'Inside voices please, I have a cracking headache,' I moaned in my best whiney tone, and locked eyes with the big man who was smiling at me. Time to sow some discourse.

'Are you the bloke they are call the Jap's Eye, then?' I watched in perverse glee as the smile fell away and gasps echoed around a very nice wood-panelled room. I really hoped my brain wouldn't find itself hanging next door by the Whistler painting (thank you, Wikipedia).

I watched the man get up and walk towards me.

'Cocky boy, ain't ya?' the King grumbled as his sausage fingers curled into a fist. I really didn't want to be knocked unconscious again. Some real sleep would be nice for a change.

'I have kept these people safe from the zombies,' he boomed. 'And what do you do? Try to assassinate me!' His voice echoed around the rooms, like so many politicians had done in the past as they explained why they had been caught with an escort, gender and sexuality dependent on the politician. But we can guess, right?

'It wasn't me, guv,' I replied. 'I was just in the area doing some scavenging.' I tried to sound convincing.

The King raised a thinning eyebrow. 'Bollocks! If it wasn't you, why did you run?' Jones spat at me, covering me in warm spittle. 'And all these houses around here are mine, so you were trespassing anyway, boyo!'

Unfortunately, I let a giggle slip out. Always happens when I'm nervous and awake.

'Well,' I replied, 'you do sound local, so they must be yours… BOYO!' And then we started a new game of kiss fist that sent me rocking back into the chair and towards the wooden and suspiciously hard floor. Goodnight, fair maidens. Sleep well.

Chapter 14

Clearly, King John Jones was quick to anger, but patient with it. Who would have known? Day after day, I was questioned about who I was and where I was from.

'Tony the Terrible,' I had replied. Unfortunately, that cost me a kick to my plums, which made me cry and wishing my mother or Olga was there to cradle me, the latter woman to kiss it better and to tell me I was being so brave, though with a hint of stupidity thrown in.

The plus side was that the bandage was now off the King's head and that had caused several deaths around the place, I had heard. For a big booming Welshman, he had particularly good hearing, so when one of his servants whispered 'Jap's Eye is about', he was bodily thrown off the roof by said target in response. But the thing I did notice was that there were a lot of men called John and a lot of people with the surname Jones. My queries about that were ignored, as they were the ones asking the questions.

After about a week, the King stopped coming to our chats, which caused me to worry.

'We don't need the gun to say you did it,' one of the bearded gits said. 'No one else was caught in the vicinity,' and he smiled as he tucked into a chocolate bar, which made me salivate.

That was the day I saw someone that I thought was dead to me. As I was being led back to the stables/cells, a tall, lithe woman walked past us from one room to another. She wore a white cotton summer dress with low heels, her long blonde hair dancing down her back with each step. Her eyes widened as our eyes met. It was her.

'Shift it, ugly,' the bearded git number one spat, and whose body seemed to be always rubbing against mine. 'Dead man walking.'

I laughed and looked him up and down. 'Well, you're not exactly in shape, but I wouldn't say you're a dead man.' I saw the girl's eyes twinkle with mirth until git number two punched me in the guts, causing me to fart.

The guard stretched out his fingers. I swear I heard them crack, though I was trying to retch up my underpants at that point.

'Hey, sexy, want to have dinner with me tonight? Then some fun?' he said to the girl and pawed at his groin.

'My name is Olga, you stinking pig,' she said in those lovely cold tones of hers. How I had missed her voice. It sounded oddly strange now that her insults weren't directed at me, but I guess she did have a life outside my home.

The two hairy-faced men laughed as I still spluttered. From my bent-over position, I gazed at her legs that she had always kept covered up at work, damn her.

'You won't be able to stay out of our beds for too much longer, Ruski,' git number one sneered. 'Rumour has it, the Queen doesn't like your attitude. You think you're too good to be her maid, so behave or off to the bedding chamber you will go!'

Olga and I managed to lock eyes again briefly.

'If you two ever touch me, I will cut the bits off you that the women like to laugh at,' she said. 'Everyone needs a good laugh.' Her sneer was enough to almost liquidise my bowels before she continued on her journey, making both men grumble and whisper to one another. I didn't think they were talking about planning a surprise birthday party.

Eventually, I was thrown head first into the stale hay, which I had come to call home for way too long. I crawled to the wooden divide between the twins and me.

'Tony, you still alive?' said the less chatty John Stone twin.

'Just,' I replied. 'I think they are becoming bored of me. If I'm correct, that's not a good thing.' I tried to get into a position so I could hear the quieter twin better. I just wished I could see their faces. I was also still amazed about Olga and I couldn't help wondering how she had gotten here. But what a position to hold – the so-called Queen's maid!

There was a brief silence until John began to speak.

'I'm afraid your time will come to an end soon, Tony,' he said sadly. 'They keep on pushing us to join their work groups. We have been given a choice of death or slavery.' I then heard what I thought was his forehead hitting the wooden partition. 'We have no choice but to agree. That's where Jim is right, about agreeing to their terms,' and he hit the wood again. 'From what Jim hears, you are not long for this world... sorry, Tony!'

'It's okay, buddy,' I said. 'It's been a tough road since it all went to shit. I have managed to dodge death many times.' I chuckled darkly, my eyes closed. I began to have flashbacks, especially the episode of me wearing the stunning red dress. Thank God that bloke was dead.

Sleep fully claimed me after that little dream episode...

...All the different emotions and stress had taken their toll on me. I awoke to the sound of doors opening and closing, shouts, and screams – just the usual noise of a post-apocalyptic Bastille. Plots and plans ran through my mind. I smiled as one idea solidified and became real all at once. All I needed was a bit of luck.

My cage door was opened by the bearded idiots. Their smiles faded as I jumped up and sprang at them, pushing my forehead into one of my captors' faces with a very satisfying crack, as his nose was spread across his hairy face. The bloodied man fell back as his legs gave way. That allowed me free rein to throw a punch at his colleague's face. Yes, it hurt me, but I guess it hurt him more. I followed that up with a kick to the side of his knee, sending him screaming to the floor.

I searched them both for the keys, before mentally kicking myself and ran to the cell door and withdrew the bunch of keys from the lock. I then quickly moved to the door to the twins' cell and struggled to find the matching key, telling them it would all be okay. The door finally creaked open and I saw the smiling pair looking at me. This was my first time looking upon them.

'Ready to leave, boys?' I asked as I gazed into the dim room. I saw two tall blond lads who were nothing more than skin and bone. They nodded avidly.

In a flurry of movement, we placed the bearded and unconscious guards in our separate cells, then locked the doors, keeping them apart and secure. After smiling nervously at each other, we did a runner. With a stroke of luck, we made it into the sunlight but drew suspicious looks from the work gangs. Ignoring the workers and walking side by side, we headed towards a large wooden gate that seemed to be devoid of guards.

I looked across and smiled at the two lanky blond-haired twins. They were smiling goofily at me. It helped to keep the nerves at bay.

'We're going to make it, boys,' Jim or John said happily, and then his chest burst open, covering the gravel with blood and bone – amongst other things that should never be seen in the light of day.

'RUN!' I shouted. However, as my feet gained purchase on the gravel, I realised I was alone. I spared a quick look back and saw the other twin gazing down at what was once his brother. He was stunned. But before I could even open my mouth to call him, he followed his brother into the afterlife, as his head was kicked back by the bullets that took away his life.

The world became a blur as I picked up speed. The screams and shouts that echoed around the grounds meant nothing to me. I would not die on a stage for some mad Welshman. If I was going to die, it would be on my own terms. My thoughts drifted to an image of Olga in that dress. I had only ever seen her in jeans or leggings. I had never seen her legs, let alone seen her in a dress. I was forced from my reverie by what felt was a punch to the back, driving me face first into the very painful-looking gravel.

'Shit!' I spat out a tooth. The pain was something I had never felt before. I was finding it hard to breathe.

Somebody then kicked me hard in the side, which flipped me onto my back.

'Arrrgghhh!' I cried out, as a new wave of pain flooded my system. I was surrounded by guards. It was then that I saw the bald Welshman. He was smiling broadly, as if he had just won the lottery. He was wearing golden robes, and in his hand was the biggest handgun I had ever seen.

'Look what we have here, boys,' the King said mockingly. 'Didn't get far, did ya, you little fucker!' Such diction.

I tried to shrug, but the pain convinced me never to move again. 'Fuck you, Jap's Eye!' I forced the words out through my broken teeth, then chuckled as the big man's face went bright red. Unfortunately, it made me laugh even harder, sending blood over my face – and, more importantly, the King's trainers.

Pain pulsed throughout my chest. I never saw the gun being raised, or even heard the noise as I followed the twins into darkness...

***

'Wake up,' came a voice, which I thought was strange. *Should I start to apologise for a life of sin now?* I wondered. *Or wait til they call me on it?*

'Will you fucking wake up!'

I shot up and realised I was still in my cell. Two blokes I had never seen before were standing over me.

'Who the fuck are you?' I said. The two men looked at each other and grinned.

'We, my friend, are Jim and John the Stone twins,' said one of the men, who I guessed to be Jim, as he jabbed his chest with a thumb at the first name. 'I know what you are thinking. You thought we would look alike, being as we're twins. But you, my friend, need to know that not all twins look the same.' I knew he was right.

'True,' I said, 'though I am quite surprised that you are different colours. Your twin brother seems...' I held my hands up to placate them, just in case they were offended. 'John does seem to be... err, black!'

The so-called twins looked at each other and laughed. 'He's discovered our secret, Jimmy,' chuckled John, who looked from side to side, clearly nervous. 'We gotta go, though.'

'How the hell did you get out?' I said. 'And please say it's dark outside. It didn't work out too well for us in the daylight.' I then realised that I was telling them about a dream, in which the Stone twins had been killed… Thank God it was that one and not the other, super-secret, dream that I won't even write about.

The twins looked at each other. 'we are on their work Gangs now, I stole the cell key' Jim stated and waved it 'Shit, man, did they hit you hard or what?' They both then helped me up, allowing me to internally scream. My knee would never bloody heal. 'Let's get out of here first, then we can talk at length.'

I had to admit Jim was right, so I followed him as he had what looked like a map. It must have been in the early hours as there were only a few solitary guards walking around the building. Those were taken care of quietly thanks to a heavy chair leg that John had found. Those guards would need help to tie their boot laces in the future.

We were crouched over a guard who appeared to have left this astral plain. Jim opened the door that the man had been guarding and John and I carried the now leaking body into the room, as we figured it was best to keep any bodies out of sight, as they did tend to look suspicious. What was leaking, I hear you ask? I did not know or care to find out at that moment in time, thank you.

John turned on a lamp, which bathed the room in mediocre light. The room had rack after rack of guns. The twins stared at me as I took in the sight.

'By the power of Grayskull,' I stated and the twins, who weren't twins, guffawed at my film reference.

There was everything from air rifles to army and police issue guns. We were like children in a candy shop. Jim looked towards me.

'What should we take?' he asked.

I chewed my bottom lip. 'Let's stick three of those army guns into that bag over there,' I said, pointing to a large canvas bag in the corner of the room, 'and as many loaded magazines as possible.'

As John went to fetch the bag, I began to pick out three sawn-off shotguns. That's where I found my old faithful, the one with the stock still attached.

'Hey, baby!' I smiled. I turned to Jim. 'Grab as many shotgun shells as you can.' I scanned around and saw belts of said shells hanging up. I grabbed three belts and put one around my waist, and handed the other two to the busy boys.

Soon, John was carrying the large bag of SA80s – as I believed they were called (thank you, Colonel) – and ammo, along with the sawn-off shotguns, a belt of ammo slung around him. He'd be sweating if we had to run.

Jim had a rucksack full of shotgun shells, along with the accompanying guns. I had a few belts and a couple of other sawn-offs stuffed in my bag and carried my old favourite in my hand. We were just about to head back out into the darkness of the corridor, when I saw a bundle of what looked like flares on a shelf. My face ached as an idea came to mind.

Jim was out front, following the map that someone had apparently given him. Even for a novice like me, the security was bollocks. Yes, they had guards on the gates, but that was it until daylight, which suited us fine. I followed the so-called twins through some outbuildings, where there were a few more guards out and about, but from the noise they were making I could walk past singing 'Don't Fear the Reaper' as I moonwalked and they wouldn't notice. That made our lives easier as we played follow the leader into a very dark building, which had bike upon bike lined up. They were the type that had chased me down earlier, as well as a few quads and two trucks.

I kicked myself for not having a knife to pop all the tyres of the vehicles we would leave behind. Our leader then pointed us towards the back of the yard, where a concrete road dipped downwards into darkness. Had an audience been watching they would be shouting out to the plucky 'Tony the Terrible' not to go there, as it would lead to certain death.

'Jim, what now?' I whispered as we hid behind one of the trucks, just as a couple of gossiping guards ambled past. Our heads banged together in the shadows.

'This is their secret entrance,' Jim chuckled. 'It's never guarded. That way, the zombies won't smell food through the door… though there ain't much brains around here.' He tucked away the map. 'Plan is to get down into the scary dark place and open the doors, then come back and push the three quads down and start the fuckers and scarper before we are shot to death.' I suddenly had a flashback to my dream and the death of the twins and, finally, me.

We all looked at each other. Thankfully, it was dark, so we couldn't see the look of fear on each other's faces. However, a question did pop into my mind. How could Jim read the map in the dark?

I shrugged. 'Hey, what's the worst that could happen?' I said. 'We've gotten further than I ever thought we would. So c'mon boys, let's hit the road, silly bollocks.'

I knew luck was with us for once. And, with a smile on my face, we headed to freedom. An image of Olga was in my heart, and my truest hope was to see her again… in that dress.

Chapter 15

'FIRE! FIRE IN THE BIG HOUSE...' '

'ESCAPE! ESCAPE!'

'Jesus Christ! What the bloody hell is going on?' Jim shouted as we pushed the three quads down the slope, hopefully to our freedom. The screams came from the panicking guards as flames licked from the manor windows. If the prime minister ever returned, he would be pissed. I chuckled as I watched the burning seat of power of the Welsh King Jones. May he rot in hell.

John saw me smiling at the burning building and looked like he was about to question me, but I didn't have time to explain what part I had played in torching the joint.

'Flares are a wonderful thing,' I mouthed to the twin to which he nodded.

Just as the first quad made it to the now open metal doors, we started to receive incoming fire. Luckily, it was as dark as an incontinent miner's knob so they couldn't get a lock on us.

'Get the bike running!' I shouted as the bullets ricocheted about the tunnels, striking the door with bright sparks. John was the first one to get his bike ready, the bag of goodies already strapped to the luggage rack on the back of the bike. He was soon followed by his mythical and paler brother. I was being tail-end Charlie. This all happened in a matter of seconds. Thanks to Jim for a quick lesson on how to start the bloody things, all I had to do now was follow the red light in front of me and try not to kill myself.

It was then that we found ourselves with company, but of the dead variety. Once again, luck was on our side as the drive from the secret tunnel was uphill, meaning that all the deadheads were gathering up speed as they moved downwards towards us and didn't have enough reaction time to grab us tightly – though there was some inappropriate touching by one or two of them. Naughty zombies.

I must admit, the guards caused their own demise as they came bursting out into the dark countryside with powerful torches and guns blazing, giving the trees hell. That, in turn, brought the overly eager, hungry and very smelly deadheads to them. The last glance over my shoulder saw them failing to close the door in time. The manor house was now breached. I prayed for Olga and all those who had been forced into servitude under that damned Jap man.

We didn't stop for what I estimated was about an hour and managed to get a good speed going along the road. The moon was high, so vision was good. However, soon enough John pulled off the road into a driveway of a largish, overgrown house. The bikes slid on the weed-covered stone-cladded drive that curled around to the back of the property, and that was where the engines were finally turned off. The boys and I sat around as the sun started to rise, all sporting big grins.

'Well, that was exciting,' I chuckled at them.

The bike engines began to make pinging noises as they cooled down. I saw John looking over at me and then into the distance. I thought he was going to have something dramatic to say about our escape – you know, something that I would remember for the rest of my life at quiet moments, and to tell my kids and grandkids as they gathered around my deathbed. I waited with bated breath, trying to hold in my excitement of this red-letter moment.

'Shit, my arse is killing me,' he moaned and launched himself off the quad. Okay, so I was wrong.

We carried the guns and ammo from the bikes into the kitchen, along with some food that the boys had collected before freeing me, and it was all placed on the dusty kitchen table. Surprisingly, this house had been left untouched. There was still some food in packets, as well as tins of varied yummy items. As the boys checked upstairs, I took my gun with me to check outside. There was a lovely sandstone-built two-car carriage. Both said cars were gone and, by the looks of the tread marks that weaved about on the concrete floor, they must have sodded off in a hurry.

The garden was overgrown, which was the norm these days, but at least it had a high wall all around its perimeter and it was devoid of all things living and dead. The only thing was a rabbit run, which was overgrown with grass and covered in ragged bits of bone and fur. You had to feel for all the pets of the humans who were left to die as their masters left them to save themselves. I managed to push the quads into the garage, while turning them around ready for a quick getaway if needed. However, as there was only one way in and out, it would be messy.

By the time I was back in the house, the boys were removing sofa cushions from the frames and were heading outside with them.

'Dusty as fuck, mate,' said Jim. 'Thought we'd give them an airing.' He threw one at me, which I dodged as my ninja-like skill kicked in. But the second hit me squarely in the face as my abused ribs prevented me from moving too quickly, and all thanks to the fists of my captors. Oh, and the ride on the quad bike; body friendly it was not.

'Come on, old man,' said John. 'Sooner we get this done, the sooner we can rest.' And so I followed Jim's so-called brother out into the crisp morning air.

I groaned as I picked up the rogue cushions. My captors had truly done a real number on my poor, abused body. As we battered the hell out of the dusty cushions, my thoughts wandered to the whereabouts of my rucksack after being a test dummy for my first ever trampoline flight and whether I should retrieve it.

It took a thirty-minute session to get the cushions suitable for our purposes. As the twins placed them back onto the frames, I opened three cans of Coke that I had rescued from the stinky fridge. After all this time, it was a real assault on the senses. To complete the breakfast, we ate cold baked beans. Separate rooms tonight, methinks. We all moaned in satisfaction while the sofa springs creaked as they took our weight. The food, if you can call it that, was devoured in silence apart from the odd belch. John played mother, albeit an ugly one, and took the empty tins out and placed them in a black bin bag, which he found in a kitchen cabinet. It's the little things that make you remember the better and safer days.

Once again, we allowed our bodies to relax as we watched birds fly about outside the large picture window, clearly enjoying themselves. Then I turned to Jim. He and John both sat on a large sofa, while I chose the smaller two-seater one.

'So, who's going to explain about the map?' I watched as they looked at me, then each other. The matter had confused me, as it was only Jim who had left the prison cell and had met the person in question, unless he made it himself, which I doubt. 'Come on, boys. Spill it.'

'Well,' began Jim, 'when I was dragged out and being instructed in the rules and punishments about our upcoming duties as the King's newest and most handsome slaves, this tall, blonde bird came past me and palmed me a note.' At that moment, my breath hitched as I knew who Jim was referring to. He explained what she looked like and it was definitely her. 'It was only when I was back in my cell that I looked at the note. It said she would visit that night, but that you were not to be told who she was.' They looked at each other and then John handed over a wrinkled envelope.

'She gave us this,' he said. 'Said it was for you.'

I looked at it and smelt a faint whiff of her usual scent, which smelt divine and all the altercations we'd had over the years came flooding back. I still hadn't opened the envelope. It was then I knew why the boys called themselves twins – they had talked nonstop, even finishing each other's sentences. I was guessing they'd only been that quiet before because of the guards. It was like having the Weasley Twins from the *Harry Potter* books on speed. They were about the same size as them, too – though Jim was blonde and John was black, as well as bald.

Without them even noticing, I stood up and walked back outside and sat on a dirty wooden bench, which creaked as I sat down. The envelope was sealed by some tape, but was still easily opened, so I read it in the quietness of the English countryside.

Tony

Where the hell have you been? I am surprised someone as lazy as you have survived, but I am very pleased you did and that I got to see you again, even though I found myself in a less than desirable place.

I was visiting a friend in Aylesbury when, as you say, the shit hit the fan. After my friend was bitten, I tried to make my way back home and to make sure you were OK. After all, if I didn't look after you, who would? We need people we can trust. I was captured while looting, but thanks to my looks I was put to office work, as the pig liked to look at pretty girls.

Even though these boys are annoying, they are your best chance of escaping. And, if I am right about the three of you, you will leave nothing but chaos in your wake, which should allow me to escape.

If we can make it out, I shall meet you in that small pub, the one where we had that lunch once after I took you to hospital that time following your rollerblading attempt. I hope to see you soon. You don't have to bring the idiots, but it's your choice.

Love, Olga

P.S. Don't fuck it up.

That letter alone brought a song to my heart. I felt nothing but hope and a possible future. But what to do with the terrible two? I could still hear them chatting away. I remembered the pub where Olga and I had once sat down together. I had bought us a nice lunch and we had shared stories of how we grew up. It was then that I started to have hopes for us as a couple. Although my antics at home always disgusted her greatly, luckily I was no longer that man… kind of.

There was a big hubbub as I walked back into the kitchen and saw John and Jim playing with the rifles that we had stolen from the King. It was clear to those who reside in heaven and hell that these boys should never have been given a weapon to hold, let alone use. At this moment in time, angels and demons would be moving themselves far away from us, as the twins didn't have a clue. Not that I had substantially more experience than them, but thanks to the long, lonely nights reading the Colonel's books, I had slightly better than no idea. I was pulled from my revelry as Jim slammed in a full magazine of ammo into his rifle.

'STOP! Do you boys know how they work?' I barked, a bit more aggressively than I had meant to. A flicker of anger shot across their faces, though not for long. However, it was enough for me to notice and worry about.

'Nah, not really, Bruce. How hard can it be?' Jim said happily in a crap Australian accent as he waved the gun around, though the barrel was pointed skywards. 'Do you, then?'

I sighed and picked up a gun from the bag. 'I haven't used one, but I have used other rifles and read about them in army manuals,' I stated and saw a sarcastic comment coming my way. 'And I've seen too many people die because they didn't treat them with respect.' I was so glad that Luger was long gone. My scar still bloody hurt.

The twins looked at each other and a fraction of a nod passed between them.

'Okay, Rambo. You show us,' Jim joked.

The twins then watched like a hawk as I slammed home a fresh magazine, pulled back the charging bolt and clicked off the safety catch. Thankfully, the manuals were up to date and I didn't look like a wanker. Then I reapplied the safety catch, pressed the magazine release and pulled back the charging lever to send the lone bullet into the air, where I caught it. The boys' faces were a picture. I was honestly surprised that it worked so smoothly, as I imagined it blinding me.

They put the SA80s back onto the table and waited for me to teach them. They were quick learners, though they never shut up, always bantering with each other. However, Jim was the only one to outwardly talk to me. John would just say the odd word and converse with his brother from another mother. After a couple of hours, we had the loading and reloading thing down pat, and then we did something I'd read as dry firing. The most difficult part was all three of us working out how to clean the weapons and then getting them back together again, while hoping that there were no bits left over – which was harder than you could ever imagine.

Finally, as the sun started to go down we were ready to begin using the guns. We all agreed to do this in the middle of nowhere, just in case the King's forces were out and about trying to find this little band of troublemakers. I had found some candles under the kitchen sink, so we ate a very romantic meal for three under the flickering light.

'So, what caused the manor to go all haywire, then?' asked Jim. 'They were shouting fire.'

A faint smile graced my face. 'That, I'm afraid, would be my fault. I didn't want to leave all those weapons for them to use on us, so I chucked some flares onto the spare uniforms.' Clearly, it might have been the wrong thing to do. If the twins had wanted to jump me then and there, they could've done so. My body was still knackered from the beatings I'd sustained. 'I thought it was for the best.'

John nodded. 'Fair play. Got a bit tricky there, though.' He looked at his brother, who smiled. 'We should have done the same.' He then relaxed with a can of Coke.

I didn't think this was over, not by a long shot. Their personalities had done a full 180. It was very predatory, and I think I was the prey.

Silence echoed around the place for a good while, until the boys leant in and started to chat quietly with each other.

'Maybe we could clear some houses? The three of us?' Jim said with a big smile. 'You said you did that with your mate, the one who died? Dave, I think you said?'

I smiled at the memory of the unlucky man. 'David, he liked to be called David,' I answered, but nodded. 'Yeah, we can do that. But it is dangerous.'

The boys' smiles grew wider, a bit like the shark in *Jaws* when Quint's feet slide towards its open maw.

'Let's get some rest, then,' I added. 'We can go out first thing tomorrow.'

The boys nodded in agreement and I headed upstairs with my weapon. There was no way in hell I would sleep without it. Slowly, I turned over a mattress in the master bedroom and threw myself, face down, onto the bed. Every bone was aching, but sleep still claimed me like a long-lost son. It was a fitful night's sleep filled with images of David's death, then my own and Olga's. Let's be honest, after that I might never sleep again. The boys were still chatting away at a mile a minute, their voices filtering throughout the house. But at least I was out of that damned manor house.

For the first time in a long while, I heard a cockerel crow in the distance. Could that mean someone else was alive? Or was it just the Bruce Willis of chickens? There were no other noises, especially in the house, which was suspicious as the boys could never shut up. With my gun at the ready, I crept down the stairs. I was thankful the staircase was so well made, as there was not a single creak as I descended. With my pulse racing, I entered the lounge to find it devoid of all things breathing. In fact, the whole house was cleaned out.

I ran out to the garage, my body hurting like crazy. I found my quad there, but all the wiring had been trashed and a note was laid upon it which read *Thanks for the help, later loser… the twins of terror.*

My teeth creaked as I gritted them. I had nothing, except whatever I had on my back. The rifle had only one magazine, and I had no food or water.

'MOTHER FUCKERS!' I screamed and began searching for a sacrificial zombie to kill. As nothing decided to turn up to allow me to kill it, I started to smash up the kitchen, and then the lounge, then anything that got in my way.

Chapter 16

There was sod all in the house – no clothes that fit, nothing to drink. So when I headed out, I was without hope. The biggest hit was the quad; even if I knew anything about electrics, it was an impossible task. The twins had ripped it apart like Freddy Krueger at a sleep clinic. Luckily, it was a cool day, so I made a start by checking that all the roads were clear first. As I began walking, I noticed a house sitting back from the road, about quarter of a mile away. That, then, was my goal for the moment. You need goals in life, even if they are stupid and small.

With my boots thudding upon the failing tarmac, I kept my eyes and ears open. The world was silent apart from the crunching of my feet. As I approached the house, I could see it was a largish thatched cottage painted pale yellow. I placed the rifle into my shoulder and levelled it, moving forward slowly. I left the safety catch on, just in case a survivor popped out to say hello. The windows were closed, and there didn't seem to be anything moving about inside, so I skirted through the overgrown front garden and down the now broken-up stone flagged pathway. Nature was really claiming back the world, big time.

It was a heavy, wooden front door, though the kitchen door was weaker with the top half being just plain glass. I lowered the gun and gave the door a loud knock and, thanks to the calm, clear day, it echoed throughout the neighbourhood. I could see the key was still in the lock on the inside of the door, so it was an invite for Mr Rock to go flying through, and what a bloody racket it caused.

I walked back out to the roadway and scanned down both lengths of the road via the scope that sat on top of the gun. It was still clear. There was nothing scaring the birds or animals from the woods that backed onto the property, which was a good sign as it meant there were no walkers heading this way. I reached in through the shattered window and turned the key. It took extra force, as it hadn't been used in many months.

I stepped cautiously into the kitchen and looked around at the dusty work surfaces. There was a disgusting smell from the things that had once been fruit, but which could now be described as penicillin. Yuck.

I dared to look in the fridge at first, but thankfully it was barren. I had come to miss the little light that welcomed you in while you made your choices. Sad times. The cupboards contained a few tins, though they were out of date – but what wasn't nowadays? Well, apart from spirits. I started to open the windows as the air did smell foul – and not just the typical staleness that you tend to find in abandoned houses. This was the smell of a lingering deadhead.

The stairs creaked like a mother fucker announcing myself to the world, though when I thought about how thick the walls were I told myself I should be okay. I eventually found the source of the smell as I pushed open a yellow, wood-panelled door and was hit fully in the face with it. There, on the bed, were two forms that once would've been called human beings. They lay side by side with their arms interlinked, with a photo of a younger family resting on top of them. My eyes filled with tears as I took in the scene and noticed a letter and an empty tub of pills on the bedside table. How many people throughout the country – the world, even – had decided to end it themselves than suffer in this shitty world? I couldn't blame them.

I wiped my eyes and closed the door. 'Damn allergies,' I muttered and wiped my nose on my sleeve.

As I walked towards the small window at the end of the hall, I heard CRACK! CRACK! My body hit the floor as the sound of gunfire lit up the countryside. *Ow... bloody ow.* I crawled towards the stairs and, like I had done many times as a kid, I slid down them on my stomach, but this time with a British Army issue rifle in hand instead of a stick. What a difference a few decades make.

I span around in the garden, trying to locate where the shots had been fired from, but the sounds were echoing around too much. Damn valley. It was then I heard a truck – no, several trucks – racing past the cottage. My eyes widened in shock as, in the back of the first one, standing proudly, was the one and only bald bastard... the King. And he was standing behind a big FUCKING MACHINE GUN.

I threw some tins of food, bottle of squash and a bottle of flavoured water into a plastic carrier bag and took a mouthful of painkillers, thanks to the old dears. Together with the fully loaded SA80 infantry rifle in one hand and the carrier bag in the other, I half ran, half limped out of the cottage and headed down the road following the noise of the trucks. Clearly, the King and his merry men had been searching for us, and if the bullet fire had been the twins firing off their guns, then they had led the crazy bastards straight here.

It wasn't long before more guns joined in the cacophony of gunfire. As I drew closer, the noise began to lessen, which didn't bode well for the virgin shooters. I turned the corner and saw three trucks in a car park in front of a post office. The King was still behind the machine gun, with another six or seven men scattered around. They looked like they had been through the ringer, all burnt and covered in blood. It was then I saw the twins on their knees, with hands on their heads. I truly was surprised that they couldn't hear the death rattle that was coming from my lungs. Stamina I have not.

'WHERE IS THE OTHER FUCKER?' boomed the wordsmith that was the King.

'WE DON'T KNOW. WE LOST HIM WHEN WE RAN!' It was Jim who was doing the bullshitting. 'HE SET THE PLACE ON FIRE. HE'S MENTAL, I TELL YA.'

I frowned as I silently crossed the road and hid in a front garden, away to the right and opposite the post office. That way, I could see everything that was going on as they continued shouting at each other about little old me. This was the best place to be, but time was of the essence as the King had now pulled out his shiny chopper. I realise that is not the best description as it brings a lot of other images to your deranged mind, though that is your shrink's problem, not mine. But that's what it was – a polished machete.

This wasn't going to end well for anyone, especially if the twins decided to join forces with the King against me. Okay, I didn't have a reason to save them, but I had to. They were people that I knew, and Olga knew them briefly enough to help them and, in turn, help me to escape. If this all went wrong, I might never see the beautiful, yet stern and disapproving, Russian woman again, but needs must.

The trouble was, at this angle it was too easy for them to scatter and hide behind the trucks – well, Land Rovers or some other bloody variant. The Welsh wonder was still ranting like the Humungus from *Mad Max 2*. You know, the big naked dude with the mask?

Leaving the noisy carrier bag behind the garden wall, I did my best to crawl behind the house. It would've been a bad day had a deadhead been anywhere near me at this moment in time – or, in fact, a horny dog. That would not have been fun. Thinking of that, I realised I hadn't seen any dogs. Yes, I had killed a few cats… by mistake… seriously. But, when you think about it, the canines would stay and fight for their masters, whereas cats would just yawn and go on holiday. There's a reason why they guard the Egyptian underworld. Even ghosts fear them.

The way was clear and the god of vengeance was on my side, as the back door of the house was wide open. The kitchen floor was covered in leaves and rubbish from winter. I tried to stay as low as I could, but my knees were quite resistant to the position I was forcing them in. Tough shit. Man up, joints – we have a job to do. The stairs were surprisingly quiet as I walked up them, while nervously playing with the safety catch on the gun. I just wished I had been able to test fire the bloody thing. That was the twins' fault, though.

The front bedroom had a musty-smelling double bed and a disgusting yellow bedspread. Not only that it, but it had bloody yellow walls. Imagine waking up with a hangover in that room on a sunny day? Jesus, that would make me want to heave. Anyway, back to the task at hand. The window was PVC framed and double glazed. I pulled up the latch; there was some slight resistance, but not too much to speak of. Thankfully, Jap's Eye was now standing on the bonnet of the Land Rover, waving his chopper around (machete, honest). He was still screaming obscenities at the so-called twins, their eyes as wide as saucers in fear. I was surprised they weren't kneeling in a puddle of warm fluid.

I slowly pushed the bedroom window open wide, hoping nobody would notice. Luckily, the King's soot-covered minions only had eyes for their victims and the bald bastard. I moved the yellow-padded seat from the yellow-painted dressing table – this room was giving me a migraine. I then placed a small towel along the windowsill. Guess the colour? Yep.

I rested the barrel of the gun on the towel and placed the stock into my shoulder. It felt weird having the magazine behind the hand grip and trigger. Not that I was an expert, but that's just how it felt. I looked through the small optical sight and saw the little red dot on the vast back of the King. Yes, it felt cowardly, but what else could I do? Wear a red bandana and go screaming down the road to slap him on the cheek and request a duel?

The charging bolt was pulled back and a bullet slid into the chamber. The sound of metal on metal echoed in the yellowest of yellow rooms. However, it was drowned out by the King's rantings. My pulse was racing as I spied on the man who wanted me dead. And for what? For trying to kill him, and possibly killing a lot of his followers and destroying his home? Some people just won't let things go.

My breathing was slow and focused as the gun sight stayed on the man's back. It was a big target. There was no chance of a head shot – yes, there was a bit of glare off his chrome dome, but that wasn't what made me hesitate. This weapon had not been tested, so I was not confident that the sight had zeroed in.

I scanned around looking at the other men, who had the look of blood lust about them. They had eyes only for Jim and John. Their guns were pointing down and no longer at the boys. Their lord and master was still bellowing at them.

'Tell me where the seedless little goat fucker is!' I presumed he meant me, but the closest thing to a goat I had slept with was a girl whose nickname was Billy. And that wasn't because she looked like Billy Piper; it was because she'd slept with a ginger bloke who looked like that Evans bloke.

The safety catch was clicked off and, with one last glance to check that the gun was on single fire, I was ready to go. The red dot was dead centre on his back. It gently moved up and down slightly as I breathed. I couldn't miss from this elevated position. Finally, the time came as I exhaled and I squeezed the trigger. The gun jumped, the stock pushing into my shoulder as the accelerant in the cartridge was ignited, sending the bullet of death spinning down the rifle barrel and into the country air, the noise hitting my ears and making me wince.

I regained my senses and saw the big man falling forwards, screaming as he did so. Everyone just stared at him. I could no longer see the lump as the Land Rover was now in the way. I quickly changed the shot selector to the three-round burst setting and focused on my next target – a tall, thin man with straw-coloured hair who had started to raise his shotgun at the boys. With a squeeze of the trigger, his chest exploded sending him and his gun to the ground. With that, the twins were on the move. Jim was going for his SA80 that was resting on the concrete and John for the shotgun, which he used instantly to start dispensing justice.

A fat man tried to run back down the road, but he couldn't outrun my bullets, which overtook him via his chest. The rest of the King's men had scattered, hiding behind their vehicles. The windows in the house that I was in were starting to spiderweb, then shatter as rounds came in, forcing me to back away. As I did so, I heard the boom from John's shotgun. With a feral grin on my face, I moved to the smaller bedroom next door (thankfully, not yellow), flung the window open and, before they could react, I focused on a man covered in tattoos. The look of terror on his face would stay with me for a good ten or fifteen minutes when he saw me and realised that my death bringer was pointed directly at him. The first two shots missed, allowing him to swivel. The third obliterated his hand, making him fall to his knees while cradling his hand. The next three shots blew out his back, which wasn't pretty. I decided that anybody who admits to enjoying this sort of thing is either mental or lying. It was a waking nightmare.

Then it fell quiet, apart from the voice of the man who should have been walking in the Welsh valleys and singing about daffodils and sheep. I still had a few bullets left, so I headed down the stairs, shouldered the gun and left the house, while trying to maintain cover wherever possible. There were bodies and blood everywhere. Some dead, some on their way. Jim and John were crouched behind a truck, looking up at the house I had just left. They were searching the windows. I kneeled down under cover and sighted in on them.

'Guns down, boys,' I said loudly but calmly. 'I don't want to shoot. But point those things at me, and we will have problems.'

'Tony? That you, mate?' Jim answered, searching for me.

'Yep, the bloke you left with no bike, food or ammo,' I answered sharply. 'Now, put your guns down, and we can have a chat.'

Jim went to raise his gun, until the better half of the so-called brothership grabbed the barrel and pushed it back down while shaking his head. Jim huffed and rolled his eyes and they both put their guns onto the bonnet of the vehicle where the crying fat fucker had once stood. He now lay in a couple of puddles, one red and the other... well, guess the colour of the day. I watched them step back, keeping their hands at shoulder height, allowing me to move out of cover, my gun still pointing at them.

We stared at each other as I walked up with my gun pointed directly at them. 'You fucked me over, boys,' I growled angrily. 'You left me with nothing.'

'I'm sorry, all right?' said Jim. 'But it's dog eat dog. We fucked you before you had a chance to do it to us.' However, there wasn't much weight to his argument. 'But I guess we were wrong. Sorry.'

It was then that I saw the King and I wanted to puke. I had missed his back totally. He clearly was dead from blood loss, but my face paled as I saw the damage my bullet had done. John nudged the man with his foot.

'Looks like your bullet went through his lower back and blew his family jewels off,' he said calmly.

'He was a dick, anyway,' Jim chuckled and gave the big man a kick. He then looked up at me. 'Thanks for saving us, and I am sorry about doing a runner. Hope you don't hold a grudge?' He looked around at the bodies. His false brother nodded avidly in agreement.

I looked at them sadly. 'No, I don't, but I can't trust you anymore,' I said and watched as they looked downcast, but they knew what they had done. 'I'm going to take this truck,' I added, indicating to the Land Rover with the machine gun on the back, 'and will be going that way.' I pointed down the road towards my goal and, hopefully, Olga. 'So please go another way. Stay safe, and only shoot if you have to. We don't know who is out there. Got it?'

'Yes, sure, Tony,' Jim uttered, while looking at the machine gun with envy. However, with a nudge from his brother, his eyes moved elsewhere.

With the truce called, we searched all the bodies. I reloaded my gun and threw some magazines into the truck, along with any food or water the King's men had brought with them. The last job was to fill the truck and bikes with fuel from the abandoned ones. With a bit of luck they would all be petrol. A couple had cans of fuel in the back, so the twins had one and I stored the rest in the back of my truck with whatever was already there, mainly boxes of ammo for my gun and the machine gun.

I threw a couple of blood-spattered SA80s in the back before walking up to the twins.

'Look, thanks for getting me out,' I said with a smile. 'Sorry it went sour. But stay safe and find a place to live your lives out. And save your ammo.'

John hugged me, and then Jim shook my hand.

'I hope you find that Russian bird again, mate,' said Jim with a wry grin. 'She was hot… scary, but hot.' He then sat on his quad as his brother from another mother started his quad up. 'If you have any kids, name them after us,' he added and gave me a shit-eating grin, before tearing off down the road.

'Like hell I will,' I muttered, grabbing my bag of goodies from behind the garden wall. Returning to the truck, I climbed into the driver's seat and took out the bottle of flavoured water from the bag. I cast an eye in the back and looked at the booty the men had brought. My heart stilled. I picked up the packet and, with a quick movement, I opened it, filling my nose with a divine smell. I dipped my hand in and crunched down on the corn snack.

'Oh, Jesus, can life get any better than this?' I said as I picked up another pickled onion Monster Munch and stuffed it into my mouth. I was in heaven.

Chapter 17

I drove for the rest of the day until I could find somewhere off the beaten track where I could park. I found a country pub that had been looted dry – though, what I did find in the Spread Eagle Inn was better than gold.

'Result!' I shouted to the heavens as I looked upon the landlord's bathroom. Not only was it clean, there was a full sixteen-pack of three-ply toilet paper. I dropped to my knees; they had heard my prayers.

Thinking quickly, I remembered seeing a water butt in the back garden just off the main car park, which I could use to get the toilet workable. As quickly as I could, the search was on for a bucket. As soon as I laid my hands on the much-needed receptacle, my bowels started to cramp.

'Oh no, not now. Please…' I moaned as I tightened the most important muscle in my body at this time.

With water from the bucket gushing down my jeans, I made my way upstairs, sweat coursing down my face as the battle of the clean underpants was on – though, clean was a matter of negotiation. Let's just say the crackle of said pants was not hurting my ears quite yet.

The water filled the cistern, and then the basin, before the axis powers in my pants made their final push. I cast away my belt like a professional stripper and dropped and squatted on the ceramic cradle of life. Those were the worst minutes of my apocalyptic life. Never trust an out-of-date tin of pilchards, especially when you are driving. The plus point was that the bathroom was comfy, empty and the previous users of this fine throne had left me a copy of the *Hobbit* to read.

'Sweet!' It took several chapters before a negotiated peace was activated. It was nice to hear a flush again and I thought back to the Colonel's house.

The pub itself had been cleared of anything useful. Even the bloody dartboard and beermats. I really didn't think the latter items would be on my list of what I needed to survive the Zombie Apocalypse – maybe I was just doing it wrong? Strangely, however, the pub landlord's apartment was untouched. There were cans of food that were edging on the use-by date, which made my bowels rattle with anger. Stranger still were the six two-litre bottles of water. This man lived in a fucking pub and he drank water. What was wrong with people!!

However, I calmed down when I found some clean boxer shorts in his drawers, along with clothes that didn't quite hang off me. With a smile on my face and a song in my heart, I took some shower gel and stripped butt-arse naked in the overgrown pub garden and scrubbed myself raw, including the valley of woe and tears. The cold water was rather soothing down there if I were to be perfectly honest. I couldn't meet Olga with a dirty arse. I am a gentleman after all, despite what you have read and learnt about me in this book.

It was while I was giving my babymakers another good clean that I heard a noise that sent a shiver down my spine. It was like a roar that was building in force and I knew it well. The horde was coming this way. Wearing only a pair of new trainers, I moved as much as I could from the truck to the pub. However, moving a heavy machine gun, tackle out and as naked as the day I was born, was not on the cards today. I figured that the car park at the rear of the pub should give some protection to the gun-carrying vehicle.

I locked the Land Rover and then proceeded to secure the pub, closing all the curtains as I went. I sneaked up to the ripe-smelling first level and closed the windows and curtains. After donning a pair of boxers, I crept to the lounge and opened the flowery curtains a crack and saw a mass of dust being pushed this way. The gunfire must have drawn them on this way. Damn the Jap Eye king and the twins.

From my time at the Colonel's house and the farm, I had learnt that, if they can't see or hear you, and they can't get in to where you are, the zombies will just carry on like a tsunami of despair and, like a boulder, they will just roll on past. They were approaching once more and the smell alone made me void whatever was left in my stomach. Even though the windows were closed, the mass groans coming from the now rotting corpses made me feel like I was sitting in a whirlwind. It made me want to scream and never stop. Not once did it let up, as the sound carried on through the night. I swear I did hear some screams, but I couldn't be sure. Even if I did, what could I do? Bodysurf over to the victims to save them? Fun idea, but no.

The wave of zombies continued for two days. The air was thick with the moans and groans of the dead and the smell infused itself into my skin and core. I found myself lying in the main bedroom covered in duvets, anything to stop the noise. It was beginning to test my sanity.

I woke up early on the third morning as the sun shone through the cheap curtains. To my joy, the sounds of the countryside could be heard once again. Songbirds were trying to outdo each other and even a pheasant joined in.

After pulling back the curtains, I stared out the window in shock. There was nothing but desolation. Shrubs, hedges and even cars had been destroyed; it looked like a picture from the battlegrounds of the First World War. Body parts and scraps of clothes were cast asunder. The only signs of any so-called life were a few crawlers who were doing their best to keep up with the horde.

With a heavy heart, I headed to the back-facing window, expecting my hopes to be dashed. But, so slap my arse and call me Jessie, I discovered that the deadheads had never made it round to the back of the pub, as there it stood like a beacon of hope, my gun-toting truck.

'Oh, thank you!' I said and rested my forehead on the cold glass. My thoughts went out to the twins and Olga. Had they made it to safety? Deep down, I knew my possible ex-Russian Special Forces maid had made it to the pub and was awaiting me with her arms open wide.

I claimed another towel as my own and, with a sponge and shower gel in hand, I headed into the garden again to have a wash. As I lathered up again, the irony wasn't lost on me that I had tried to get to the town of Aylesbury to find company and protection, only to have to go all the way back again to meet up with my darling Olga. Well, she did say 'Love' in the letter. That had sent my heart souring, and my loins a-tingling for naked fun times… if she allowed me, of course. If not, then my dream version of Olga was a lot more accommodating.

After a breakfast of Monster Munch and water, I started up the beast of a truck and let it idle for a bit, while I just sat and stared out over the stunning countryside. The one thing I was proud of during this time was not only staying alive despite the beatings, that accursed dodgy knee, and my pilchard-eradicated bowels. It was that I could now drive. Yes, it had taken a while. And yes, I still hit things – the odd car, phone box, and the bungalow in the last village… Who knew they could jump out at you like that? Crazy days.

Like I had said, the road was strewn with rubbish of all manner of things, but thankfully it looked like the walkers were starting to degrade under the sun's heavy gaze. Maybe over the next few years they would finally be gone from this land? That led me to start wondering whether this was happening all over the world. Could human beings make a comeback? However, it had been a very long time that any kind of air traffic had been seen, so maybe it would take a bit longer. The plus point was that the world did smell better for it, unless you were driving over fresh corpses. My heart went out to them. After all, they had once been people; they'd had families and friends before this plague had descended on us.

The downside to my musing was that my concentration had waned, making my driving a little erratic, though thankfully the truck wasn't too badly damaged as I reversed it out of the shop window. Take that, health food shop! I was back on the road and I had a destination in mind. The loneliness of the world was weighing down upon me. So many lives had been lost due to this outbreak and I didn't even know where and how it started. All I had cared about at the start was myself and my treats. What a shallow and selfish man I had been back then. Hopefully, I had changed enough for Olga to like me. Maybe I shouldn't mention all the people I had killed.

I stayed overnight in an abandoned garage; the shutters were difficult to use, as you had to pull them up manually via a chain which tore at my hands. It was worth it, though, as it gave me a safe place to sleep and I could drain the cars of fuel and top up the petrol tank of the truck. It was not surprising how much petrol the bloody thing used, especially as the roads were so full of crap from the deadheads. The thing had hardly gone over twenty miles per hour. I was feeling full of hope, as tomorrow I should be able to make it to the pub known as The Moody Cow. I hoped the Russian beauty would be happier than the cow.

The dreams I had that night changed from borderline filth to slasher horror. I knew that, whatever happened, I had to get to my destination the next day or else I would go out of my mind. So, as the sun broke cover in the morning, I had a quick wash and was just about to start off, when a thought entered my head. *What if I caught up with the horde?* My eyes looked up at the machine gun and grinned.

The next two hours were spent slowly unloading the gun, taking notes on a pad of paper that I had taken from the garage office. Then, I slowly managed to take it apart and clean the bits with the gun-cleaning kit the twins and I had stolen from the manor. Then I reloaded it and put a round in the chamber, having tried some dry firing first. It was my time spent at the Colonel's house that had paved my way to survive this, otherwise my weapons could've blown up in my face. Apart from that damned mass murderer of a Luger, I was the only one to walk away from that thing.

Back on the road it was slow-going. Any crawlers were dispatched via Dunlop power. As the miles were covered the road widened, which meant I could go faster and my heartbeat gathered to mirror my speed. I saw a turning coming up that I knew would take me towards the pub. It was in the middle of nowhere, and thankfully the horde had just followed the main road rather than this one. That thought alone made my heart leap.

My excitement caused me not to notice a discarded shoe on the side of the road. It was only later that I would see the signs that my blinkered eyes hadn't assessed. As I turned around a hairpin corner that I remembered was just by said pub, I slammed on the breaks, though not quickly enough. I hit the edge of what seemed to be a mini horde. By my count, there were about a hundred or two gathered around the pub. It was then that I saw a waving hand and the blonde hair of a person at a top window. It was my Olga.

Bloody hands and maws beat at the windows of the truck. I was trapped. I tried to drive forwards and back, but there were too many. So close, but also so far. How could we die when we were in sight of each other? Fate can be a real fucker sometimes. I crawled into the back seat as the bloodshot eyes of the dead watched and rocked the truck. I grabbed one of the SA80s and smashed out the back window that led to the flatbed of the truck. It took a couple of goes, which seemed to excite the dead even more. But, with the glass removed, I primed the rifle and, with a single shot, I sent the ones at the front to hell, casting their brains into the air. Trip Advisor will not be liking this at all.

After two rounds of magazines the way was clear, but not for long. Walkers tripped over their brethren to get at me, but they were too late. Soon, I was perched on the back of the truck with my legs braced and the machine gun loaded and primed. A wave at the blonde caused a single finger to be raised. Or it was a Russian sign for good luck? It did have a smile attached to it.

I unleashed hell. After a couple of minutes and one ammo change, I was surrounded by the dead and they were staying that way. It was carnage. The truck was awash with shiny brass casings of the spent rounds and torn-up flesh. My ears were ringing like a royal family wedding. I climbed back through to the driver's seat and drove over the carnage. Thankfully, I couldn't hear the noise of the battle of skulls versus tyres. It couldn't have been nice, though we did win.

I was soon parked up at the front entrance of the pub. The walkers had lived up to their names and had walked into my killing zone, leaving the entrance clean and virginal. I slipped out of the driver's seat with the SA80 hanging across my back on a sling. Yes, I was a bit bloody now, but it wasn't too bad. My breath hitched as the door opened and my once cleaner and dream girlfriend stepped out and stood there, looking around. She was wearing jeans and a T-shirt, with her long hair pulled into a loose ponytail. She had never looked so good.

Not a word was shared as the distance closed between us. Her eyes looked me over as her fingers traced my facial scar. Her expression softened and something I had dreamt about for years happened; her lips touched mine and we kissed. It started soft and then the heat was turned up. Gasping, we pulled apart and grinned goofily at each other. Her hands cupped my cheeks and she smiled again, which was rare for her.

'What took you so long?' she asked.

The horde was coming, and we knew it. Within moments of our loving embrace, we were back on the road and starting to head back down the road in the direction I had travelled. As I drove, Olga told me about life at the manor and how lucky she was not to have been chosen to become a bed companion like so many other poor girls. Then how, with my escape and the carnage it had caused, it had allowed her to release the other prisoners and run off into the night.

I told her about how I had survived, but I skirted around a few things that would stay with me to the grave. I explained that I had left our hometown before it had been burnt to the ground, then about the Colonel's house and the farm next door. We stayed at the pub I had stayed at on my journey to her. The first night we spent in separate beds in a small room. But, as with the last time, the firing had brought the horde back onto us. We huddled down for a whole week, this time in the master bed. On the third night, we became one, and I had never been happier.

During our time lying in bed as the countryside was again taken over by the dead, we planned. And her mind was as sharp as the nails that tore into my flesh when the sun went down. When we awoke in each other's arms, with the sun shining upon us and the birds calling, we knew that we would be together forever.

Epilogue

Nine months later, our son Dougie was born. We had made our home in the farm next door to the Colonel's. We scavenged the land and managed to find enough animals to breed from. It was a hard time, but Olga's family had been from farming stock, so I followed her lead. The next year we had young cows, sheep and pigs, and not to mention the flock of chickens at the Colonel's house. We fenced it in to keep the chickens safe.

Over the months, people turned up and inhabited the other farms around the area, enabling us to trade with them. In our fourth year, our daughter Emma was born. By that time, there were over fifty people living around us and a healthy market of foodstuffs had been set up between us all. That year, we searched for metal shipping containers which we used as barricades on major roads, securing us from the roaming hordes. From the reports that came our way, we learnt that there were similar hordes throughout the world. They gathered in their numbers and just roamed, trying to flush out the living people.

As the years went by, the numbers of the dead lessened as their bodies degraded to the point where their bodies fell apart. So, when out last child, Gabrielle, was born six years after settling down, the reports were saying that the hordes had halved in numbers and living people had started to bounce back. And Olga and I were happier than we had ever been. But she still wouldn't wear that maid's uniform. I was still working on it.

The End

Coming in December 2020 from Nick James

The Time Traveling Tourist

Printed in Great Britain
by Amazon